DREAM OF TERROR

Helga Radford, child of an English
aristocrat and a German governess, comes
to Gales Hill at er dying father's request
to seek reconc tion with his estranged
family. Helga s ggles to become loving
and dutiful tov ds her autocratic grandmother but she is unfamiliar with English
ways and is n easy target for those
who resent h coming. There are stares,
whispers, lies and finally accusations which
threaten to destroy her. Set in mid-
nineteenth century Northern England, this
tale of seething, violent passions makes
gripping reading.

DREAM OF TERROR

by
Ruth Abbey

Dales Large Print Books
Long Preston, North Yorkshire,
England.

British Library Cataloguing in Publication Data.

Abbey, Ruth
   Dream of terror.

   A catalogue record for this book is
   available from the British Library

   ISBN 1-85389-651-9 pbk

First published in Great Britain by Robert Hale & Company,
1976

Published in Large Print August, 1996 by arrangement with
Robert Hale Ltd.

Dales Large Print is an imprint of
Library Magna Books Ltd.
Printed and bound in Great Britain by
T.J. Press (Padstow) Ltd., Cornwall, PL28 8RW.

ONE

It is more than two years since I left Gales Hill, but even now after all this time, the terror of what happened there sometimes haunts my dreams. And upon such nights I awake with shaking limbs and wildly beating heart, almost sick with fear until the terror fades and the blessed realisation that it is all over and that I am safe, dawns upon me.

Looking back, I think I sensed almost from the very first, that something was wrong, that it would be unwise to make my home at Gales Hill, for even then, right at the beginning, I was disturbed by doubts, strange little fears that I could neither formulate nor understand...But at the time I put my unease down to the fact that I was only eighteen and that having lived all of my life up to the last few months in Germany, was unfamiliar with the life and ways of the English aristocracy. And I was determined not to let the one distressing experience I had suffered in

5

London make me suspicious minded. For I believed sincerely, and indeed, in spite of all that happened, still do believe, that most people are what they appear to be and are to be trusted. 'One must have faith in one's fellow men.' How many times had I not heard dear Schwester Füdisch who had taught me in the Damenstift advise: 'It is the only way to live.' I knew that she was right.

And in any case, my situation being as it was, the steps I took were in truth the only ones open to me at the time. I had no alternative than to act as I did...

But let us go back to the day it all began, the day I first set foot in my grandmother's house...

It was a raw February morning, damp and depressing, that I boarded the train for the north of England. Because of my impecunious situation I had of necessity to travel in one of the truck-like third class carriages, and I was cold and uncomfortable. I could have asked Grandmother for money to be sent to me, but my pride had prevented my doing so. Although she had sought to make peace with Papa and me, I still could not forgive her, or my late grandfather for their attitude towards Mama.

As I sat chilled and cramped on the miserable wooden bench that served as a seat, I opened my reticule and took out the letter that had brought my journey about. I unfolded the thick, stiff notepaper, my thoughts winging back to the day it had arrived at the cheap lodging-house where Papa and I were living. We had been living in London just over three months when it came, months in which Papa's already failing health had steadily worsened. He had been ill, when, on the death of Mama, we had left our home in Heidelberg to journey to England, and his condition had deteriorated rapidly. No doubt the damp foggy weather in which London seemed to have been shrouded ever since we arrived, was largely responsible.

I had taken the letter to him as he lay, weak and frail, in his bedchamber. I knew what it would mean to him, for since the day, a week or so earlier, that he had written to his mother in Yorkshire, he had looked anxiously for a reply.

'Look, Papa. The letter you have been waiting for.' His face had lit up, I remembered, as I put the square envelope into his hands, and my heart had lurched with a fearful anguish at the sight of his thin, wasted arms on the cambric coverlet. He was dying before my very eyes, and I had known that it could not be long before the end came...*Dear* Papa, tears of weakness and relief had filled his eyes as he had read the words his mother had written to him, words which I now, yet once again, read for myself:

'My Dear Son,
    You and your daughter are welcome now at Gales Hill. My only grief is that you waited so long to communicate with us. Your father died ten years ago, a sad and bitter man, grieved that you did not seek to be reconciled to us. And yet I cannot find it in my heart to blame you. Angry, hurtful words were spoken on both sides, and perhaps our action seemed to you beyond pardon. To us, at the time, it seemed the right and proper course to take. Now, after all these years, I am not so sure. One grows less rigid in one's views with the advance of time. It is too late, I know, to ask forgiveness of Helga, your late wife, but perhaps the young Helga, your daughter, and you

yourself will someday feel able to forgive us.' The letter was signed, 'Your loving Mother.'

As I returned the letter to my reticule I recalled how moved, and yet agitated Papa had become on reading it.

'But I *did* seek reconciliation,' he had told me, a baffled expression in his eyes. 'I wrote from Heidelberg that day that you were born, to tell my parents they had a little grand-daughter.'

I had soothed him by pointing out that he had done his best, that he was not to know that they had never received his letter and that there was no purpose in upsetting himself over something that was past and unalterable. Now, going over the events in my mind I fell to thinking how different our lives might have been if my grandparents had received Papa's letter, and to wonder what had become of it. No doubt it had been lost or destroyed in some mail-coach disaster or in a Channel storm, I decided. It seemed the most reasonable, in fact, the only explanation.

The train rattled and clanked across the countryside. Here and there labourers in the fields stopped their tasks to gaze, round-eyed as we passed. The railroads, Papa had told me, were being received with mixed feelings by the people of England, and it was clear that by many of them they were regarded with a mixture of suspicion and awe. Mrs. Binks, for instance, the lodging-house keeper, viewed them as the Devil's own invention.

'Nasty, smoking tea-kettles, racing about,' she would say indignantly. 'I wouldn't ride in one not for Queen Victoria herself!'

I smiled as I recalled the dire warning she had sounded upon learning that I was to travel to Yorkshire in such a manner. She had wept when I had taken leave of her, convinced I am sure, that I was going to my doom. Poor Mrs. Binks, such a worthy little woman, compassionate and kind. She would for ever hold a place of affection in my heart for her goodness to us during those last days. Papa had died the very day of receiving Grandmama's letter. After reading it, he had asked me to promise that I would go to Gales Hill and make my home there.

'It is your rightful place,' he had urged me.

'Of course, dearest Papa,' I had agreed. 'We shall go together just as soon as you are well enough to travel.' He had smiled then, at peace at last, and had replied that, yes, that would be the best plan, to go together. And then we had tried to keep up the deception that last afternoon, that Papa would recover, but we had known, both of us, that when I did embark upon the journey to Gales Hill, it would be alone: that Papa would have already embarked upon another, greater journey, his final one...

Seconds before the end, he had opened his eyes and looked directly into mine. 'Promise that you will go, Helga.' The time for pretence had passed.

'I promise, Papa,' I whispered brokenly.

He had known that I did not truly wish to go to my grandmother, but he had known also, as I did myself, that short of taking on some menial occupation, it was the only course left to me. I could not live for very long on the meagre amount of money that there was for me, and my chances of obtaining a situation even remotely suited to my position in life were extremely improbable, Mrs. Graham-Lewis would see to that. Since our coming to London, I had been employed in this lady's house as a seamstress. The situation had been brought about through Mrs. Binks whose daughter Fanny was a scullery maid in the Graham-Lewis mansion. On her afternoon off one week, Fanny had told her mother that 'the mistress' was in need of somebody to undertake some fine needlework. Mrs. Binks at once approached me. She had noticed, she said, some of the stitching I often worked at, and wondered if I might consider the position.

'Begging your pardon, I'm sure, Miss Radford,' she had apologised. 'Perhaps I shouldn't 'ave said nothink, seeing as 'ow your're a lady, but...'

Dear Mrs. Binks, I knew exactly what she was trying to say, poor soul! I was a lady, but obviously in reduced circumstances...how otherwise to account for my father and me residing in her lodging-house...I had been both touched and grateful and had gone at once to be interviewed. Mrs. Graham-Lewis had been impressed by my sewing and had given me the position. It suited me well because I did not have to live-in, could attend to Papa in the mornings and evenings. Papa had not been too happy about the idea but I had begged him to allow me to occupy myself in this way at least until such time as his health improved and he himself could support us more comfortably.

At first all had gone well. Though I did not greatly care for Mrs. Graham-Lewis herself, I enjoyed the employment she gave me. The clothes and household linens I was required to mend or adapt were without exception of the finest quality and it was a pleasure to work upon them. She herself was of reasonable prowess with a needle and this accorded a certain feeling of affinity—properly lessened by the difference in our respective stations in life, of course—between us. Her husband, it transpired, was by birth a Yorkshireman, a circumstance which I believe contributed in no small measure to my father's allowing of me to take the position. What dearest Papa did not know, nor I myself at the outset, was that Mr. Graham-Lewis was a philanderer. He was extremely personable to look upon, and appeared to be a considerable number of years younger than his wife. She herself was a large woman, very plain of feature, and I must confess to having wondered what had drawn the two together.

I had not been employed in the house more than two weeks before he began paying attention to me, but I kept out of his way as much as I could and fully believed that my manner would cause him to desist from such folly. But one day when I was mending a morning-gown of my mistress's and believed myself to be alone in the house, he strode into the sewing-room, grabbed my arms and kissed me full on the mouth...At that precise moment his wife walked in. She had returned earlier than expected from a carriage drive. I protested my innocence, of course, but to no avail. The husband uttered not one single word in my defence. I think his wife knew, or guessed the truth of the situation, but no doubt it lessened her sense of outrage and humiliation to lay the blame at my door. Poor woman, I almost pitied her until she made her scathing reference to Mama. I should have guessed she would from the patronising air she had assumed on learning from me earlier that Mama had once worked as a governess.

'I might have known,' she almost screamed at me. 'I might have known what to expect from the daughter of a common governess.' At once pity gave place to anger.

'My mother was a lady,' I retorted. 'Gentle and kind, beautiful, in fact, both of nature and in *appearance.*' Very wickedly, for I had been taught both by Mama and by the Sisters, that adverse personal remarks were ill-mannered and unkind, however subtly phrased, I laid great emphasis on the word appearance. The barb went home and I had the satisfaction, sinful though it no doubt was, of seeing the tell-tale colour suffuse my employer's uncomely face. I was, of course, dismissed on the spot and without references. Papa was bitterly angry about the matter but because of his illness unable to do anything about it. I made light of the situation and talked blithely of getting another position, hiding from him the sense of outrage I had felt at the injustice I had suffered. Both he and I had known the outcome. Mrs. Graham-Lewis was well known and powerful in society. She lost no time in poisoning people's minds against me. The doors of all the great houses were closed to me.

It was this state of affairs which had driven Papa to write to his family. Fear of what was to become of me after he had gone overcame his pride. And with the approach of death, the desire to make peace with his family, and to have me acknowledged by them had outweighed all other considerations. Nothing could change the past. There was no purpose to be served in dwelling upon it and harbouring resentment. It was the future now that must be looked to.

The train was slowing down and I realised that we must be approaching the market town which was as far upon my journey as I could travel by train. It looked, I thought, a bleak, windswept place, and I pulled my frieze mantle closely about me as I stepped down onto the open platform. It was becoming dark and with the approach of night, the cold seemed to have intensified. Feeling very alone, I stood for a moment wondering what to do. I had written to my grandmother advising her of the estimated time of arrival and I had hoped that she would have despatched someone to meet me. But I could see only one carriage about and two ladies, first class passengers by the quality of their baggage and apparel, were making towards it. I took them to be mother and daughter. The younger woman, I thought to be about my own age. She was small, dark and very pretty. Seeing me she favoured me with a blank stare from her large velvety eyes. There was no smile, no inclination of the head in response to my own overtures. Lifting her fur cloak, she began to climb into the waiting carriage.

'Oh look, Mama,' she said in a voice loud enough for me to hear across the platform. 'There is a third class passenger alighted here, she must be a new servant for the Hall, I suppose.'

Furiously angry I felt my cheeks burn. The mother turned at her daughter's words and glanced towards me. Even in the dimly lit station there was no mistaking the expression on her face. She was staring at me as though she had seen a ghost. Then quickly recovering she followed her daughter. 'I expect so,' she agreed. 'Perhaps Mr. Southwold has hired more staff whilst we've been away.'

They drove off at once and still smarting from the insult I approached the porter and informed him that I was expecting a conveyance being sent from Gales Hill. Had he received a message concerning delay, perhaps—or any message at all for

Miss Radford. At first he stared at me blankly, then the name Radford seemed to bring him to life. At first I had great difficulty understanding him for I had no knowledge whatever of the Yorkshire dialect, which was, I presumed, what he was speaking. It sounded, accustomed as I was to the speech of London, almost like a foreign language. But I gradually was able to make out that there had been no message for me at all. It was a pity, he went on, that I hadn't 'Said summat afore; happen t'ladies that had just gan would've taken me as they went past t'very spot.'

Personally, I thought such a thing highly unlikely and in any case would not have wished to ride with them.

'Is there a gig or vehicle of any kind for hire?'

He shook his head. 'Nay, Miss. Nowt.'

'How far is it to Gales Hill?'

The man pushed back his cap and scratched his head. 'I reckon it'll be eight or nine miles as t'crow flies,' he replied.

My heart sank. Eight or nine miles! What was I to do? I would not relish the thought of walking such a distance at any time, let alone at night and along strange country roads, roads that were perhaps rough and hazardous. But I could not remain where I was. Making a quick decision I decided to set off to walk. No doubt I should meet the carriage from Gales Hill very soon. Grandmama would be sure to have despatched one. I would take my trunk to save having to collect it at some later time, I told the man.

'Very good, Miss.'

'Which way is it?'

He pointed out the direction I was to take. I wished him goodnight and stepped out into the night. From the first the ground began to rise, gently at first then more steeply. Struggling for breath in the keen night air, I battled on, determined not to give in to the nervousness that was already beginning to assail me. The gradient of the hill grew ever greater and soon the only thought left to me was that of gaining the summit. Just as I reached the top, I heard with blessed relief the sound of horses' hooves and carriage wheels coming up behind me. I staggered onto the grass verge, waved and shouted then fell in a heap to the ground....

TWO

The next memory I have is that there seemed to be a hammering in my head, a bewildering confusion of sounds and feelings that held no meaning for me. Then out of the noisome murmurings and babble, words formed. I heard them at first as though from a great distance.

'Who are you? Where are you going?' They sounded faint and far away and although I could hear them quite plainly, as yet they made no sense to me and evoked neither recognition nor response. I had no part in them. Again they came, louder this time, nearer, more insistent, and through the mists in which I drifted, their meaning finally reached me. Slowly, with difficulty, for it seemed as if some great weight pressed down upon my eyelids, I opened my eyes. I stared at the white blur above me, a blur without shape or form. Then, as the shrouds in which I had lost myself released me to consciousness at last, I saw that it was a face. A man was bending over me. Grey eyes were looking searchingly into mine.

A tremor of alarm seized me. Who was this man? And where was I? Struggling to sit up, I looked anxiously around for some clue as to my surroundings and saw at one that I was in a carriage of some sort. Then remembrance came rushing back. Of course! I had swooned just as I had heard the sound of a vehicle approaching. I stared at the stranger now seated opposite to me, wondering with a little trepidation what manner of person he might be. The apprehension I felt must have shown in my eyes for I was at once reassured that there was nothing to worry about.

'There is no need for alarm,' I was told. 'You are quite safe, I assure you. But now that you have opened your eyes at last, perhaps you will enlighten me as to what a waif like yourself is doing wandering along country roads alone and in darkness?'

At the stranger's words, much of my unease left me. I had not, as I had at first feared I might have done, fallen into the hands of some ruffian or foot-pad. This man was obviously a gentleman. His speech was that of an educated, cultured person, and his apparel looked to be of the finest quality. The interior of the carriage too, testified to wealth, with its soft velvet cushions and fur knee-rugs. All the same, gentleman—and one of means too, though he might be, I did not feel completely at ease with him. There was something in his manner that seemed to upset me: a high-handedness and arrogance of tone that I found unnerving. He had certainly not addressed me as an equal. No doubt, I reflected miserably, my air of poverty had not escaped him. He must have noticed how threadbare my mantle was, how worn and shabby my gloves and kid boots. No doubt he took me for a servant or other such person of humble station. Assuming an air of confidence that I was far from feeling I explained the situation and told him where I was bound for.

A look of impatience crossed the dark, handsome features.

'It was an extremely fool-hardy way to behave,' he rebuked sternly. 'What on earth possessed you to act in such a manner? You might easily have been robbed–or worse...'

I blushed, conscious of his meaning, and looked quickly away from him.

'I expected to meet the conveyance

from Gales Hill almost at once,' I said defensively.

'In which case,' he argued smoothly, 'it would have been much more sensible to await at the railroad station until it came, would it not?' I did not reply. In my heart I acknowledged the reasonableness of what he was saying but I was angry at the way I was being lectured. 'Did it never occur to you to put up for the night in the hostelry?'

'No. It did not. And I am still sure that someone will come to meet me.'

The man regarded me through narrowed eyes.

'I can see,' he announced to my great surprise and discomfort, 'that you are almost as stubborn as you are beautiful.' The remark was so outrageous, so unexpected as to render me speechless. I felt my face suffuse with colour again. 'However,' he went on, 'there is nothing to be gained in sitting here all the night.' He shouted to the coachman to continue on the journey, and the carriage moved forward. I started up in alarm.

'Where are you taking me?' I demanded. 'Please tell your man to stop at once. I wish to get down.'

'Indeed, and I shall do no such thing,' came the bland response. 'My house, to which I was peacefully proceeding until... until you erupted upon my vision so dramatically, lies in the same direction as your destination. You will remain in my carriage until the vehicle you are so sure of, arrives from Gales Hill. This is the only road, we are bound to meet it when and *if* it arrives.' Aware that he was quietly making fun of me, I made no reply. This to my further discomfort appeared to amuse him.

'Oh dear,' he began with mock dismay. 'I do believe I have offended you. Pray forgive me, my dear young lady. But as a magistrate of this county I really cannot allow a helpless female like yourself to wander abroad on lonely roads by night; my conscience will not let me.'

Stung by his tone, I was at first tempted to reply indignantly that I was not helpless, not by any means. And then I changed my mind and decided to reply in the same coin. I would show this haughty aristocrat that it was no servile domestic he was dealing with.

Assuming a falsely sweet smile, I remarked:

'I am relieved, dear Sir, to learn that you *have* a conscience; one can never be *quite* sure...' As I spoke I had the intense satisfaction of seeing a look of surprise flit across his face. But he was not be to outdone.

'Ah,' he retaliated with an irritating grin, 'spirited as well as beautiful: an interesting combination if I may say so...'

He was looking at me now with unconcealed boldness in his eyes, a boldness that was almost insulting. The man was insufferable, I decided. Close to tears I prayed silently for the Gales Hill carriage to arrive. Desperately weary from my long journey, angry and humiliated, I felt I was near to breaking point...

Then suddenly, the carriage began to slow down. I looked from the window and saw lights in the near distance. My heart lurched sickeningly. This must be the man's residence and I had no intention of being taken there. I began to get up, then sat down again as the vehicle swayed to a standstill. From without came the sound of voices and general commotion.

'What the devil's going on out there?' The stranger sounded impatient. The coachman appeared at the carriage door.

'It's t'carriage from Gales Hill, Sir,' he announced.

A second man appeared immediately behind him. Poking his head inside the carriage and doffing his cap, he addressed the stranger:

'Begging your pardon, Sir,' he began. 'I've come to meet Miss Radford from t'station down yonder. Briggs said as 'ow you'd—' he broke off and looked from one to the other of us.

'I am Miss Radford,' I told him, getting up.

A look of surprise quickly followed by one of annoyance flashed across my carriage companion's face.

'Why did you not tell me who you were? he demanded.

'Because,' I replied evenly, 'you did not do me the honour of telling me who *you* were.'

'Touche! I am Edward Southwold—at your service.'

There was a glint of admiration in the man's eyes as he held out his hand to me, which served as a salve to my wounded pride.

The Gales Hill coachman was apologising for his late arrival.

'One of t'osses went lame and I had ti gan back and yoke up t'other, you see Missie.' He spoke in the same dialect as the man at the station and although I got the general gist of what he was saying I did not fully understand him. My bewilderment must have shown on my face.

'You will soon become accustomed to our Yorkshire dialect,' announced Mr. Southwold. 'That is, if you plan to remain in the county for any length of time.' It was, I considered, an astute way of asking me how long I was going to stay at Gales Hill. Perversely, I decided not to indulge the questioner.

'My plans are a little uncertain at the moment,' I replied vaguely.

We were walking now towards my grandmother's carriage, just a few paces from the one we had left. I saw that we were immediately outside the pair of huge ornate gates, beside which stood a small gate-house. An old man was busy opening the gates. A woman, presumably his wife, carrying a lantern hurried beside him. She curtsied to Mr. Southwold. The old man touched his cap.

'Evening, sir.' Then, almost in the same

instant the two of them looked towards me. I was about to step into the carriage but something in their manner arrested me. A gasp, instantly stifled, had escaped the woman's lips. I glanced at her sharply but she turned quickly away. I looked across at the old man. There was a look of bafflement in his watery blue eyes and he was staring at me with an intensity that was mildly disturbing. Mr. Southwold taking his leave of me appeared not to notice.

'Goodnight, Miss Radford. My respects to Mrs. Radford.'

'Goodnight, Mr. Southwold. Thank you for assisting me so gallantly.'

I was being deliberately rude and my sarcasm made its mark. Anger flashing in his deep grey eyes, Edward Southwold bowed, turned quickly away and climbed into his carriage. When it had disappeared through the opened gates and thus moved out of our path, the driver turned my grandmother's coach round. The old couple were still standing about, watching. Passing close to them as we turned I heard the woman say:

'I tell you it must be. T'same blue eyes, t'same hair—gold as corn—she's Fraulein's daughter I tell you.'

'Then there'll be trouble,' muttered her companion. 'You mark my words, Martha, trouble and—' I heard no more as the coachman, with a crack of his whip and a shouted 'Goodneet' to the two of them, set the horse for the road again.

A flicker of unease stirred within me. What had the lodge-keeper meant by his strange words, his talk of trouble? Grandmama had requested my presence at Gales Hill. She must wish me to be there. As we drove along I pondered and puzzled over the matter. The old couple had obviously known my mother—or someone like her. My likeness to her was, as the woman had perceived, quite remarkable. I knew of course that Mama had lived for a time at some large residence in the vicinity of Gales Hill. This must have been the one, Edward Southwold's. But clearly he had not recognised me at all.

Then it dawned on me that if he had known Mama he would have been only a child at the time. He was, I estimated, somewhere between twenty-five and thirty years of age and it was some twenty odd years ago that Mama and Papa had eloped. I smiled to myself at the thought that

Mama might have been Mr. Southwold's governess all those years ago. Thinking about the man, I half regretted that I had spoken rudely to him. After all he *had* come to my assistance and perhaps I had misinterpreted his manner. He had behaved with a marked lack of respect, it was true, but on the other hand he had done me no harm. And it was plain to see that his employees—at least the three I had encountered—held him in quite high regard. Could it be that I had over-reacted to the boldness in his eyes? Perhaps the behaviour of Mr. Graham-Lewis had made me altogether too sensitive and suspicious. I must guard against such a reaction, I reminded myself.

In a sense, I was at a loss to understand myself. It had been a relief to me when grandmother's carriage made its belated appearance and yet now, conversely, I felt out of sorts with myself as I rode along in it. Irrational and completely unexpected though it was, I experienced what I can only describe as a feeling of let-down... Then I shook myself irritably. Such an idea was nonsense. I was thoroughly glad to be out of the arrogant Mr. Southwold's company! I told myself I was being stupid and put it down to my extreme weariness.

The coachman had set the horses to a steady trot and as we rattled through the lonely lanes I knew that it would not be long before we reached our destination. I wished that I had asked Edward Southwold a little about Grandmama. Now that the time of meeting her was drawing ever closer I began to feel nervous. Papa had, of course, told me much concerning his mother, but he had not seen her for more than twenty years. No doubt she would have changed much in that time. From the letter she had written it seemed that she had softened somewhat with the years, and indeed I prayed that it might be so.

The carriage was slowing down. With wildly beating heart I peered out of the windows and saw that we had turned in through a pair of handsome iron gates on to a narrow, tree-lined avenue. At the end of it I could just make out the outlines of a large house with belts of trees to the north and east.

'Here we are, Miss,' shouted the coachman, drawing the horses to a halt. I opened the carriage door and climbed down. At once the full force of the wind struck me, almost lifting me off my feet. Gales

Hill was aptly named, I thought wryly, steadying myself and clutching my beaver bonnet to my head. The coachman did not linger. He lifted down my trunk and put it beside me, then turning the horses smartly round, disappeared in the direction of some outbuildings. I was alone. I stared up at the house before me. Torn by the wind, the trees around it bent and groaned, their branches twisted in grotesque and frightening shapes.

The house itself loomed strong, square and solid, impervious to the worst the winter gale could lash upon it. It breathed strength and security. And yet, in spite of this, and in spite of its associations, I was in no way drawn to the place. I had half expected, I think, that because Papa had lived there and had loved the place, I would at once feel an affinity with it: that I would automatically experience a sense of belonging. But I felt nothing of the kind. I felt what I was, a stranger.

Anger and bitterness filled my soul. Try as I might I could not forget that these doors through which I was about to pass had been for ever closed against my mother; that the arrogance and pride entrenched within them had driven my father from the place he loved and deprived him of his birthright. I could not erase from my memory the manner of his dying, if not in abject poverty, at best with little comfort. Nor could I forget that my grandmother had until now rejected me too, seemingly uncaring as to whether I lived or died. For in spite of what she had stated in the letter about wishing my father had sought reconciliation far sooner, it seemed to me that if she and my grandfather had truly cared about us, they would have taken steps to find us...there was certainly money enough to have done so...

My resentment was so strong at that moment that I wished I had not come... I felt that I did not wish to meet my grandmother at all. I wanted neither her patronage nor her charity. I told myself that to have taken on some menial role in life would have been preferable to accepting either. But there was no going back. I had promised my dying father...come what may, reconciliation with his family must be made. I must bury my pride, my resentment, as he had done and be ready to forgive. Dreading the impending interview, I made for the front door.

THREE

A maid-servant answered my summons. A cheerful, rosy-cheeked girl, bounding with health and energy. She knew who I was.

'You'll be Miss Helga,' she greeted me, round-eyed. 'And I bet you're tired out luv—waiting all this time o' that there daft Briggs—he's allus at t'last minute. But come on in luv and I'll tell t'missus he's gotten you safe here at last.' She spoke, like the other country people I had encountered, in the broad vowels of her county, but by now I was becoming a little more used to the strange-sounding words, and managed to understand her. I nodded and smiled and followed her into the entrance hall. She had picked up my trunk as though it were as light as a feather and put it down at the foot of the wide, sweeping staircase. Then she led me to one of the doors leading from the large, square hall, and having knocked upon it, threw it open.

'She's here,' she announced without

ceremony. 'Miss Helga's come, Ma'am,' and stepped back for me to enter.

A tiny figure, dwarfed by the huge chair in which she was sitting, rose to meet me. At sight of her much of my bitterness and anger melted. Could this frail little elderly lady with the faded eyes and weary expression really be the grandmother against whom I had harboured such resentment? Where was the arrogance, the stiff-necked pride I had attributed to her? It did not show on her features. She looked sad and old...in a sense, defeated. It would be difficult to go on hating such a person. The room, the drawing-room obviously from the way it was furnished, was lit by two oil lamps which stood on sofa-tables, one beneath the tall windows, the other behind the brocade couch. They were turned very low. A log fire burned in the marble fireplace and the flames cast fitful shadows across the dimly lit room. I waited, standing just inside the closed door, thinking my grandmother would make some move towards me. But to my surprise she did not. She just stood still where she was, looking across the expanse of room between us. I twisted my gloves nervously, not quite sure what she would expect of me in the way of greeting. Then suddenly she spoke:

'Well, child,' she asked, 'have you lost your tongue? Come along in and pay your respects to your grandmother in a proper manner.' Her voice at once dispelled the illusion of weakness created by her appearance. It was strong, full of command, the voice of one accustomed to being obeyed; the arrogance, the hauteur were still there all right. In a sense it was a relief to me for in spite of my earlier intentions of forgiveness, I was not ready to give up my resentful feelings. I did not want to love her...not yet. In a way I suppose, I felt I owed it to Mama, to continue to hate my grandmother, and her arrogant mode of speech was making it easier for me. The sound of my footsteps deadened by the deep pile of the baroque-scrolled carpet, I moved across the room and stood before her. She was, I saw, not looking directly towards me, but a yard or so to my left. A trifle puzzled, for there was no one else in the room but the two of us, I held out my hand. She did not take it. Her arms remained where they were, stiff and straight by her sides. It was like a smack in the face for me and I felt my temper rising. Was this how she intended to treat me then? To snub me as she had done Mama? How dare she write and say that I was welcome if this was the way she felt towards me? Hastily I withdrew my proffered hand, words of anger trembling on my lips. But before I could voice them, my grandmother spoke.

'How much longer do I have to wait,' she demanded, 'before you condescend to come and kiss your grandmother?'

From my superior height I looked down at her in amazement. And then I knew. She was blind! Totally blind! Tears stinging my eyes, I put my hands gently on her thin shoulders and bent and kissed her wrinkled cheek. I felt the frail old body tremble for an instant at my touch, but otherwise there was no sign of emotion.

'At last,' she announced in the same dictatorial tone as before. 'I was beginning to think you had lost both your tongue *and* your manners.' It was a moment before I could speak. Pity for her welled up within me. I was at a loss to know what to say. She herself had made no reference to her affliction. Did that mean that she wished for me not to do so either? Also her use of the word condescend had not escaped my notice. She had sensed immediately something of my attitude towards her. Obviously she was not a person to be trifled with. I coughed nervously, begged her pardon and murmured that I hoped she was well. She did not give a direct answer. Instead, to my surprise, she replied:

'Poor child. It has been a shock to you, to find that I am blind. That stupid Polly should have warned you.' She then went on to say that no doubt I must be weary from my long journey and in need of rest and refreshment.

'We shall talk tomorrow,' she announced, groping her way to the bell-rope beside the fireplace. 'You may retire at once, and Polly will bring you something on a tray.'

I did not demur. For one thing I was almost asleep on my feet and for another I could tell that it would be useless to resist the old lady. Polly appeared and was instructed to show me to my bedchamber, to help with my unpacking, and then to ask Cook to prepare a light supper for me. I was following in the maid's wake when Grandmother suddenly called me back.

'One thing I must know at once,' she announced. 'What are you like?'

'What am I like...?' Because I was so weary I suppose, her meaning was not absolutely clear to me. 'In what way—?'

'In appearance, of course, child,' she sounded impatient. 'Whom do you resemble, your father or your mother?' From something in her tone I sensed that my answer would have much importance for her.

'I have been told, many times,' I replied, 'that I am the living image of Mama.' I was looking directly at Grandmother as I spoke and I saw her lips tighten at my words.

'Oh,' was the only response she made. But there was no need for more. In that one word was all the disappointment in the world. In a way, I understood a little of how she felt: it was natural, I supposed, that she should have hoped for me to be like her son. As I climbed the stairs I reflected on the fact that she had not once addressed me as Helga. Always child, it had been. Did she still hate the memory of my mother so much that she could not bring herself to say the name? The thought hardened my heart against her once more.

Polly was quick, efficient and loquacious. Half of what she said made no sense to me at all but I let her chatter on. It was easy just to let her words flow over me, for as she seldom paused, there was little or no need for me to make any contribution to what in truth was more a monologue than a conversation. She obviously knew that I had lived abroad most of my life and seemed very impressed by the fact. And if it wasn't an impertinence, she would like to know a bit about 'them there foreigners' sometime. She beamed when I replied that I would be happy to talk to her on the subject, only at a time when I was less tired. I gathered, and it was agreeable to hear such news that they were all, in the servant's hall, glad that I had come to Gales Hill.

'I'll bet Mr. Francis will be an' all, when he sees you,' she went on. 'He likes a pretty face, he does, I can tell you.' I wondered whom she could be talking about. As far as I knew, my grandmother lived alone, except for the servants. There had been a ward, Emma, who had been brought up at Gales Hill but Papa had said that no doubt she would have married and moved away. He had not mentioned, as far as I could recall, anyone by the name of Francis. However, I was much too tired to question the girl on the matter, and in any case was not really interested. I felt, that night, a complete lack of interest in my surroundings altogether. I felt drained, lost in a sea of loneliness, and an aching emptiness of the heart. I longed then as I had never done before, for our old home in Heidelberg. For times past, when Papa, Mama and I had all been together, fulfilled and happy in our life among my mother's gay and friendly people. I had hated London with its leaden winter skies and choking fogs. And I felt at that moment that I hated this northern place even worse. It was alien to me, completely so. What I had seen of it seemed bleak and bare, with nothing to soften its harshness. An unfriendly place, hard and uncompromising.

I began to wonder about the people. Papa had told me that most northern people were warmhearted and kind. The ones I had encountered had been, with the exception of Polly, quite the reverse. The girl at the station, Edward Southwold, both had been disdainful in their attitude. Even Grandmama, of my own flesh and blood, had shown me less than whole-hearted welcome, and I could not forget what the lodge-keeper and his wife had said about me: that there would be trouble...

For the second time that night a finger of fear touched me. Then I reminded myself that I was not a prisoner at Gales Hill. I could leave. And go against my father's fondest wish? His dying wish? I knew that that was something I could not do. I would have to try to come to terms with my new circumstances, make the best of the situation and live in peace, if not in complete accord, with my autocratic relative. I reminded myself that Papa, in spite of everything, had loved her to the end. If he could forgive her, then surely I could also. But I would not be subjugated by her; any future bond of affection and regard must be forged and maintained on a basis of mutual respect and strength. I had no intention of allowing her to dominate me, or reduce me to a state of cringing servility. She must accept me as an equal.

Thinking on these lines led my thoughts to Edward Southwold again. He had regarded me as his social equal only after he had heard my name. He had considered me beautiful before that though, I recalled. There had been no mistaking the admiration in his eyes, respect or no.

Suddenly a picture of the dark, handsome face with the deep grey eyes and noble forehead flashed across my vision with quite remarkable clarity. I wondered if I would ever meet him again and found myself hoping that I would. Not, I reminded myself, that I had formed any liking for the man. Far from it. No, the only reason I wished to be in his company again was because he had rattled me and I wanted to get even with him. It seemed important to me that he should come to regard me as his equal not because of my family name, but for myself. Why it should matter so much to me, I did not seek to understand...

I blew out my candle and settled myself comfortably between the lavender-scented sheets, revelling in the warmth and comfort. Outside in the night the wind screamed and moaned among the trees with unabated fury and once or twice I held my breath, sure that one of them at least must come crashing to the ground. Never in my life had I experienced such a gale. I thought it must surely keep me awake throughout the night. But I had underestimated my exhaustion. The wild sounds became fainter and fainter to my ears, and then I heard them no more...

FOUR

'You wish to speak to me, Grandmama?' It was the next morning and I had been summoned to my grandmother's bedchamber.

'Yes. Sit down child.' I walked across the room and sat down in a velvet chair that was drawn up close to the great four-poster bed. Grandmama, I thought, looked smaller than ever, a diminutive figure in her lace bed-cap and shawl. She was propped up among the lace-edged pillows partly hidden from my view by the pink silk bed-curtains which had not yet been looped back to their daytime position. I asked if I should attend to the matter and she nodded.

'Not that it makes any difference to me,' she announced, 'but at least it will facilitate conversation as far as you are concerned.' When I was seated again she came straight to the point.

'I am aware,' she began to my acute embarrassment, 'that you do not like me.

I felt your resentment and animosity the moment you entered my house.' I did not at first reply. There was no denying the truth of what she said. I decided that I would be as straightforward as she was. After a moment's pause I said slowly:

'How could you expect my feelings to be other than they are? I loved my mother very dearly. I can neither forgive nor forget your attitude towards her.

'Well at least you are not a hypocrite,' she replied promptly. 'Your sincerity should provide a basis on which we can come to an understanding.' When I said nothing in reply she continued:

'What I cannot understand is why, feeling as you do towards me, you came here at all?'

'It was my father's dying wish. I promised him that I would come.'

'You yourself had no desire to do so?'

'None.' I saw the thin lips tremble at my unequivocal reply and wished for an instant that I had been less abrupt.

'Do you wish to remain here?' I hesitated, not all that certain at that moment exactly what I did wish for the future.

'I am not sure,' I returned at length. 'I

know that it was Papa's dearest wish that I should be reconciled to his family—to yourself, and that I should accept my proper position in life, and with part of myself that is what I wish but...'

'But the other half of you feels,' she finished for me, 'that in doing so you would be disloyal to your mother?' There was a gentleness in her tone that took me by surprise. She had expressed my feelings exactly.

'Yes,' I replied unhappily. 'For Papa's sake, for my own, I wish to be truly your granddaughter, to love and respect you—but oh, why, why did you have to behave as you did. Why did you treat Mama so cruelly?' I broke off, unable to continue for the sobs that shook me. Grandmama waited until I had calmed myself and then said quietly:

'If I tried to explain to you, I do not think you would ever understand. There were rules, standards in those days, by which we lived, by which all our class lived. Born in a different environment they no doubt seem to you harsh and wrong. To us, brought up with them, they seemed right and proper. Time alone can be the ultimate judge of these things. I ask only of you that you try to accept that we acted in what we truly believed, at that time, to be in our son's best interests...I...we loved him very dearly...' Her voice broke and I saw two tears trickle from her sightless eyes. At once my heart smote me. Who was I to have set myself up as judge and jury? What gave me the right to condemn without compassion or charity, without even trying to understand? I felt ashamed. I remembered the words in our Lord's prayer: that we be forgiven even as we ourselves forgive. I had recited the words glibly countless times, but now, for the first time, their meaning reached me. How small then my own chance of Divine forgiveness in my present state.

I rose from my chair and putting my arms around the frail figure in the bed, kissed her on the cheek.

'Papa forgave you,' I told her, 'and in spite of everything never lost his love for you. Now I too, though I cannot understand, will try to forgive.' As I spoke I experienced a strange sense of release, as though some weight had dropped from my heart.

'It is a wise decision.' Grandmama had recovered herself. 'One can never be happy if the heart is full of hatred or resentment, as I myself am only too aware. One cannot send another person to hell without going halfway along the road with them.' It was a revealing speech. So she, too, had suffered at what had been done. Perhaps even more than my mother and father. I thought she looked tired and strained and suggested that I ought to leave her to rest. But she dismissed the notion at once.

'Nonsense, child. I am not in the least tired,' she retorted with a return to her dictatorial tone. 'And I have not finished with you yet. You have not told me whether you wish to remain here or not.' She spoke as though the answer to her question were of little consequence but I was not deceived by her manner. Something, perhaps even the over-emphasised nonchalance gave her away. I knew that she greatly wished for me to remain at Gales Hill.

Grandmama was waiting for my answer. I had to make a decision one way or the other. She was not the type of person to be fobbed off with a 'maybe' or 'perhaps'. It had to be yes or no. Even with the beginnings of respect that were being forged between us, I had difficulty in making up my mind. The sensible, practical course of action was, of course, to stay; at Gales Hill I should live in comfort, luxury almost, and occupy a position of some social standing in the community and indeed the county. I should want for nothing, and I should be fulfilling my father's wishes. Everything in fact pointed towards remaining. And yet I hesitated, unable to dispel completely the unreasoning flicker of doubt. Looking back I know now that it was intuition, some sixth sense given to me as a warning. At the time I told myself I was being fanciful and stupid.

'I will stay, Grandmama,' I told her.

'Then that is settled,' she replied without the merest trace of emotion. 'Now, tell me about your life in Germany. There are many things I would like to know about.' I had never in my life encountered anyone so self-controlled and I did not know quite what to make of her. I was torn between admiration and disquiet as I asked myself *was* it self-control or a complete lack of feeling on my grandmother's part? Perhaps my original conception of her had been correct, after all, that she was cold and hard. She was the exact opposite of Mama, I reflected, Mama with her fierce passion and her uninhibited displays of emotion.

'I am waiting. It seems you have lost your tongue again.' Grandmama's remark brought me back from my reverie.

'I'm sorry,' I apologised, and began to tell her something of the way we had lived in Heidelberg. It came out that she knew the city.

'I visited it as part of the Grand Tour I made with my father when I was your age,' she confided. To my great delight it appeared that she had been much attracted to the place and considered it one of the loveliest cities she had ever seen. Here was one subject on which we could be in complete accord. It seemed to afford her much pleasure to relive her memories of it and we eulogised over its many beauties. Like me she had been fascinated by the castle, magnificent and fortress-like standing high above the Neckar River and the roof-tops, at the head of the valley.

'We lived fairly near to the university,' I told her. 'Papa was able to earn a little money by helping some of the students with their studies in English, private coaching, you know. It was a great help to us, and augmented Papa's small income.'

I made the remark unthinkingly and, as God is my witness, without malice, but at my words a dull red flush stained my grandmother's cheeks.

'I'm sorry,' I burst out impetuously, 'I did not mean to distress you—'

'You do not distress me,' she replied. 'Your father, like everyone else, had to lie on the bed he made for himself.' But in spite of her denial, I sensed that I had upset her and I wished I had not mentioned the subject of money. Papa himself had never complained. His parents had cut him off without a penny but he had a small legacy that had been left to him by his godmother and we had managed to live, if not in anything remotely like the style to which Papa had been accustomed, at least without hardship. The money had all gone now, of course, but at least there had been enough left to pay for Papa's funeral. Grandmama went on to ask me about father's illness. I had told her of his death of course when I had written to tell her that I was coming to Gales Hill but I had not given any details. She listened avidly to what I had to say which was that Papa had died of lung complications following a severe attack of influenza.

'Poor, dear Richard,' she murmured, almost to herself I thought. 'He always was troubled with a weakness of the chest, right from early infancy.' I was able to assure her, and I could see this was a tremendous relief to her, that Papa had not suffered unduly. She fell silent then, but I got the impression that there was something bothering her, that there was a question she wished to ask but was having difficulty in bringing herself to voice it. Suddenly, out it came.

'Was your father happy? Was your mother a good wife to him?'

'Of course,' I replied, just a trifle indignantly. 'Papa was, I am convinced of it, extremely happy. Mama was devoted to him.' I saw no need to tell Grandmama about Mama's fits of temper. I never knew what they were about, in any case, and it seemed disloyal to her to mention them. And despite the quarrels which ensured when Mama was taken this way, my parents had, I felt sure, been truly happy and in love. But the question troubled me, reviving memories that I had thought buried and forgotten. Perhaps because of my own reservations, I answered, quite rudely I am ashamed to confess, that I was surprised that Grandmama should ask such questions. I had a strong suspicion that she was casting doubts upon Mama's character. I stared into her face endeavouring to divine her meaning but the sightless eyes were as always a screen behind which thoughts and feelings could be effectively hidden.

'I did not mean to upset you,' she said. 'And your answer is a relief to me. It seems that I have worried unnecessarily all these years.' Her answer puzzled me.

'What about?' I asked quickly.

'Why, about your parents' happiness of course,' she smiled. 'What else?'

What else indeed! That was what I would have greatly loved to find out. The answer she had given me was not the true one, of that I felt certain. She knew, or suspected something of which I was ignorant. Something about Mama. It was a worrying thought. But I already knew Grandmama well enough to realise that if she had made up her mind to say no more on the subject, it would be futile to question her further. We began to talk of other things, practical matters about whether I needed new apparel, what I was to occupy my time with, etc. Grandmama insisted that I was at once to receive a dress allowance, a very generous one, and to visit her dressmaker and milliner. As she herself would be unable to accompany me, Emma and her daughter must do so.

'Emma?' I began, and then remembered. Emma was Grandmother's ward. She had been brought up with Papa. He had often regaled me with stories of the childhood they had spent together.

'Your ward still lives here?' I asked in some surprise.

'In the Dower House in the grounds,' Grandmama replied. 'She is extraordinarily attached to Gales Hill, and on her marriage somehow persuaded her husband that the Dower House was where they should reside. Indeed,' she went on, 'I do believe she would not have consented to marry him otherwise.' I somehow sensed a faint criticism in her tone.

'Obsessed with the place, she is. And I don't think her poor husband ever really cared for it—'

'You speak in the past tense, Grandmama,' I interrupted.

'Emma was widowed early in her marriage.'

I murmured that I was sorry to hear such sad news.

'She and her daughter were left amply provided for,' she announced. 'I do not know the exact extent of the fortune Mr. Lewis left but it was, by all accounts, very considerable indeed.'

'No amount of wealth can compensate for the loss of a loved one,' I argued.

'True,' she agreed. 'Nothing makes up for the loneliness.' She paused and then almost to herself, I thought, murmured: 'Although I sometimes doubt if Emma ever really—but there, I must not keep you longer. It must be almost time for luncheon. Run along, child. It is discourteous to Cook to be late for meals.'

Polly showed me to the dining-room. I had taken my breakfast in my bedchamber and this was the first occasion on which I had dined formally. A young man, whom I guessed to be somewhere in his middle twenties, was already seated at the head of the massive mahogany table. He rose and came towards me with outstretched hand. As he bowed over my own, he introduced himself.

'My dear Miss Radford, Francis Wade, at your service. I apologise a thousand times for my absence yesterday. Business, alas, kept me away from home.' I smiled and said that I quite understood. So this was Mr. Francis, who, according to Polly, liked a pretty face around. He himself was very personable to look upon. Of medium height with brown hair and eyes, his features were perfectly regular and finely moulded. Only the chin, I thought, spoiled the effect. It was less than manly, suggesting a slight tendency to weakness or effeminacy. Nevertheless, his was a face that would be attractive to a great many of the opposite sex, I felt sure. I was surprised at the way he was attired. His clothes were flamboyant to say the least and not at all what I had imagined country gentlemen of the north of England to favour. From snippets of information let fall by Papa, and indeed from Papa's own way of dressing, I had pictured them as practical, down-to-earth people, not given to 'frills' of any kind whether of dress or manner. I found myself contrasting this man's appearance with that of Edward Southwold. The latter had been elegantly dressed but in a restrained fashion, completely devoid of ostentation or vulgarity.

Suddenly I became aware that I was myself being subjected to a careful appraisal. I blushed hotly. At once Mr. Wade was full of apologies.

'Pray forgive me, my dear Miss Radford,' he begged. 'It was unpardonable of me to stare so blatantly. It is just that I was totally unprepared for someone quite so beautiful.'

It was a charming compliment and uttered, I thought, with sincerity. I smiled and inclined my head. I felt I was going to like Mr. Wade. Over luncheon he explained his position in the Gales Hill household. He was the adopted son of my grandparents. They had taken him into their home, when at the age of twelve he had lost his parents, both of whom had been well known to them and held in very high esteem by them.

'I suppose, in a sense, I helped to fill the gap left by your father,' he began, then stopped, a look of confusion and embarrassment covering his handsome features.

'I say, I'm most awfully sorry...' he stammered. 'What a damned tactless thing to say, by God...please forgive me...'

I told him the matter was of no

consequence and he seemed very relieved. As we were to live under the same roof, he went on, it would be 'God-damned awful' if we got off on the wrong foot so to speak. In future he would hold his garrulous tongue in better check.

When we had finished our meal, Francis, as he had insisted I must call him, asked if I would like him to show me over the house and grounds. I said I would like that very much, but first I must go and ask leave of my grandmother. She seemed pleased when I told her what we proposed to do. By the time we returned, she added, she would be downstairs in the drawing-room.

It was a bright day, but cold, and I wished that my mantle had been thicker and warmer. I truly was in need of new apparel and I thought gratefully of the generous allowance I was to be given. The thought of buying clothes of good quality without having to stint myself excited me more than a little, and I hoped that arrangements to go shopping would be made very soon.

Francis was a pleasant companion and obviously going out of his way to be agreeable. We made a tour of the house first and as we passed through the kitchens Francis introduced me to the other servants. They curtsied politely and as Polly had already intimated, seemed genuinely glad to make my acquaintance. The house itself was beautiful.

It had been built, Francis informed me, during the late eighteenth century, by one of my ancestors. It was large, and all the rooms were spacious and imposing and most luxuriously appointed. The family I belonged to was obviously well-to-do. We wandered from room to room, Francis pointing out this and that notable painting or piece of furniture and it was clear that he was knowledgeable of fine things. I myself had no great interest in such matters, neither houses, nor their trappings, but for politeness sake I feigned an interest I did not feel. Actually I was much more interested in my companion than in the things he was showing to me, for to me people were, and always had been, much more fascinating than things. I loved talking with people, from all walks of life, eager to hear of their lives, their hopes and fears, their aspirations and ambitions. Both Papa and Mama had often told me that I showed an unladylike curiosity in this matter, that I should be more reserved. But it always seemed to me such a waste of time, all the formalities, the pointless small-talk with which one was supposed to be content. All my life from earliest childhood I had read prodigiously, and had learned of the acute social problems confronting the peoples of many countries. I loved to discuss them, and had done so frequently with the students in Heidelberg. And had I had the opportunity I would have wished to occupy myself in working for the betterment of those in need. My parents used to tease me about my crusading spirit. I was neither typically English nor typically German they would say with mock dismay.

'Most young ladies in England content themselves with their embroidery, their music, etc., or their social round,' Papa would tell me. And Mama would add that most young German women spent their energies on becoming skilled and proficient in household duties.

'To be a good *hausfrau*, that should be your aim.'

In truth though, I do not think that they seriously disapproved of my aspirations. I think they were secretly amused by them and considered them something I would 'grow out of.'

We were outdoors now, walking through the grounds which, though not large by country house standards, Francis informed me, were none-the-less quite extensive. The Dower House Grandmother had spoken of could be seen through the leafless elms.

'Mrs. Lewis and Lavinia are dying to meet you,' my companion informed me. 'They have been spending part of the winter abroad and knew nothing of your coming here until I appraised them of the fact this very morning.'

'When did they return?' An idea had suddenly entered my head. 'Last evening by any chance?' Francis nodded.

'I believe so. I myself arrived home very late last night and in consequence cannot be absolutely sure. But they certainly came back sometime yesterday.'

'I believe then that I may have seen them,' I told him. 'A lady and her daughter left the train when I did last evening. The porter mentioned that they lived near to Gales Hill.'

'Then perhaps you would like to go over and visit with them at once,' my companion was boyishly enthusiastic, 'and see if it was indeed they.' I shook my head.

'Some other time. I cannot intrude upon them uninvited. In any case, Grandmother said she expected them to call on her later in the day. I shall wait to become acquainted with them until then.'

In my heart I sincerely hoped that the two ladies I had encountered were not Emma—Mrs. Lewis, and her daughter. If they were, I was in no hurry to make their acquaintance. We wandered on, out of the grounds and on to the road. In the distance I could see a farmstead, perhaps half a mile away, and further off on the horizon a second one. I asked if the farms belonged to Gales Hill.

'No,' said Francis. 'There is no estate with the property. Just the two houses and the park. The farms belong to the Southwold estate. Gales Hill lies just beyond it's eastern boundary.'

'This Mr. Southwold, he owns much land?' I queried.

'He's the biggest landowner in the county,' came the reply. 'And incidentally, the most eligible bachelor in the north of England. There's many a fond mama around here nursing dreams of her daughter becoming mistress of Southwold Hall, I can tell you. And come to think of it,' he continued with a grin, 'some of the old crows will be fit to scratch your eyes out when they see how beautiful you are. They'll see you as a formidable rival to their darling daughters, many of whom, let me add, are depressingly plain.' I laughed. He certainly had an entertaining manner of speech.

'They need have no fear of me,' I told Francis, 'I am interested neither in the great Mr. Southwold nor his wealth.'

'Ah, but you have not met the gentleman.' My companion wagged a playful finger. 'The ladies fall like ninepins for him.'

'Then I shall be the exception,' I replied. For some reason which even to this day I do not fully understand, I did not divulge the fact that I had already met Edward Southwold. I had not mentioned the meeting to Grandmother either, and there again I could not account for my reluctance to talk about it. I shook myself mentally and dismissed the man from my mind.

The sun had gone behind a thick dark cloud. I shivered and we decided to retrace our steps. On the way back I asked about the peasantry of the district. What did they do? How did they earn a living and so forth.

'I imagine that most are engaged in agriculture?' I suggested.

Francis nodded 'Almost exclusively.'

'I would very much like to find out something of the way English farmers and their wives live.' I went on, 'Would it be in order for me to visit some of them?'

Francis looked at me with some surprise.

'Of course, if you wish it. Though I should imagine it would be devilish dull. Most of the labourers are an ignorant, loutish lot, and some of their masters little removed from clodhoppers.' His words made me angry.

'Perhaps it is not their fault that they are ignorant,' I cried passionately. 'Have they the chance to be anything else?'

Francis was clearly startled at my outburst, and a little amused.

'I dare say not,' he laughed. 'I dare say not, but what of it? They are of no consequence, and to educate them might give them ideas above their station, I fear.'

I said no more. Clearly this was a subject on which Francis and I would disagree completely. 'Anyway,' he continued, 'it can be of little concern for someone like yourself. For beautiful young ladies there are much more interesting pastimes available.'

He gave me a roguish grin as he spoke and it was impossible to take offence. Obviously Francis did not take me seriously. Strangely, I found myself wondering what views Edward Southwold would hold upon the subject: it would be interesting, I thought, to discuss the matter with him. We were almost at the park gates when someone came up behind us on horseback. Turning I saw that it was Edward Southwold himself. He appeared so very suddenly that it almost seemed as though my thoughts of him had conjured him up out of thin air. For no apparent reason I felt flustered and slightly nervous, wondering how he would greet me. But I need not have worried. For he did not stop or dismount. He merely gave a brief bow in my direction and the briefest of nods to Francis, as he rode by us.

'The mighty one himself,' whispered my companion. Then feigning great surprise:

'But you are still upon your feet! You have not swooned!'

I could not help but laugh merrily at his jesting. He really was an amusing person. In spite of my laughter, however, I felt just a trifle put out at Mr. Southwold's cursory acknowledgement. True we had not been on the best of terms when we parted the previous evening, but surely he could have afforded me the courtesy of dismounting and passing a civil pleasantry or two. Then I told myself it was of no consequence. I cared not a fig what he thought of me, or how he behaved towards me. But my feeling of pique remained just the same...

FIVE

We arrived back at the house to find Mrs. Lewis and her daughter in the drawing-room with Grandmama. To my dismay, the two ladies were indeed the ones I had encountered at the station. But their attitude towards me now was vastly different from that of the previous evening. When Francis had made the formal introductions, Mrs. Lewis at once apologised for not having spoken to me at the station.

'We had no idea that you were coming here,' she explained, 'otherwise we should naturally have invited you to share our carriage.' I replied that I had expected no such favour from them; I was after all, a perfect stranger.

'All the same,' went on Mrs. Lewis, 'I ought to have realised. My wits must have been dulled by all the travelling we had done. I should have known at once whom you were, and I do beg you to forgive me, my dear.' She took my hand and kissed me warmly on the cheek.

'Actually, it bothered me all the way home,' she went on, 'the fact that I couldn't place you, I mean. You reminded me of someone, but I couldn't for the life of me bring to mind whom it could be.' She spoke with seeming sincerity and yet I felt she was lying. I believed that she had known instantly that it was my mother, and for some reason had been upset by the knowledge. Why otherwise should she have blanched so?

But as etiquette demanded I remarked that I knew exactly what she meant and that I had experienced the same frustration on occasion.

Lavinia reiterated her mother's sentiments.

'When Francis came over this morning and told us of your arrival and we realised our mistake, we felt so ashamed,' she began. 'Mama, in fact had to reach for her smelling-salts and—'

'Well it was perhaps more from over-fatigue that I needed them,' put in her mother swiftly, 'the journey you know—'

'Oh, I don't think so, Mama.' The large violet eyes were wide. 'It was not until Francis said the name Radford that you went so white—'

'Did you have a reasonable journey, Helga?' Mrs. Lewis cut her daughter short. 'I have heard that the behaviour of some of the second and third class passengers is quite coarse, their language and jests often disgusting. I trust it was not too painful for you.'

I replied wryly that the only things I had found painful about my journey were the cold, and the hardness of the wooden seats.

'To think that we could have mistaken anyone so beautiful as you for a servant,' Lavinia, in spite of her mother's obvious efforts to change the subject, returned to her theme. 'But it was rather dark, if you remember, we didn't see you at all clearly... and as you had not travelled first...' her explanation trailed off miserably and I felt sorry for her. I had thought previously that given the opportunity I would revel in getting even with this young lady, but oddly enough I felt no desire to do so. I found myself liking her. There was a candour, a certain naïvety about her that was quite charming. To put her at ease I enquired about the Grand Tour and was rewarded with a spate of excited chatter. The two had visited several places in Germany with which I was familiar. They had been, they told me, particularly enchanted with the Rhine Valley.

'The castles perched high above the river are *so* romantic-looking,' Lavinia enthused, 'like something from fairyland or a dream—'

'But did you meet a *prince-charming* in any of them?' It was Francis who asked the bantering question. Lavinia flushed, but before she could reply, her mother answered for her.

'Lavinia has, I believe, aroused the interest of a prince-charming much nearer home,' she said coyly. 'And I doubt if even the magnificent Rhineland Schlösser could produce a more noble one.'

'Mama, please...' the poor girl was clearly embarrassed, but her mother was not to be silenced so easily.

'Lavinia is too modest. She thinks I am being presumptuous—'

'And are you?' It was Grandmother who asked. Mrs. Lewis was swift in her denial.

'No,' she replied, and it was evident that she was annoyed. 'I am not. One can always tell when a gentleman is interested—'

'Please, Mama, pray do let us change the subject,' begged Lavinia. To come to the girl's rescue, I turned to Mrs. Lewis and told her that my father had often spoken of her to me.

'With much affection, I may add,' I concluded warmly. 'Truly he regarded you almost as a sister.' I thought the remark would please her and I might have supposed that such was indeed the case had I not been looking directly into her face as I spoke. For even though her involuntary reaction to my words was swiftly veiled, I was aware of it. Anger, had flashed for a second in her blue-grey eyes, anger quickly replaced by smiles and sweet words.

'Oh yes,' she returned, *'Dear* Richard and I were just like brother and sister together almost from the very first day I came to Gales Hill, as your grandmother will confirm.'

'Indeed you were,' replied Grandmama. She sighed. 'Ah, what happy days those were...'

'Now we mustn't go dwelling on the past,' put in Mrs. Lewis firmly. 'What is important is the present and the future. Looking back too much is of no benefit, Aunt Louise.' It was the first time I had heard her address my grandmother in this fashion and my bewilderment must have shown on my face.

'Oh, we are not truly aunt and niece,' she explained. 'It was just that we "adopted" the relationship. It was convenient.'

Over tea, Mrs. Lewis explained more fully to me her position at Gales Hill. Because of Grandmama's blindness she had taken over most of the responsibility of running the household for her.

'I come along every day, at some time or other, to satisfy myself that everything is running smoothly and that Aunt Louise is well.' She went on to say that it had troubled her a little, leaving my grandmother for so long while she and Lavinia visited Europe, but she had given full instructions to the servants before she left and had had an assurance from the local vicar and his wife that they would look in at Gales Hill as often as possible.

'A promise which they kept to the letter,' she added. 'Such a splendid couple.' She went on to tell me that the Reverend Sykes and his wife had newly come to the area from the south and that they lived in the parish to which Gales Hill and its environs belonged. The previous incumbent had passed away some months earlier and Mr. Sykes had been appointed in his place.

'Perhaps he is a little too liberal in his views,' she continued, 'but none the less a credit to his calling. Mr. Southwold made an admirable choice.'

'Mr. Southwold chose the vicar?'

'Of course.' She seemed surprised at my asking. 'Who else?' Then seeing my look of bewilderment, *'Dear* Mr. Southwold is patron of the living here.'

'Indeed,' I murmured politely, still not quite sure what she meant.

Just then Lavinia and Francis who had been conversing together with Grandmama, joined us on the window seat, and we began to speak of other matters.

Just before they left us, Mrs. Lewis took me on one side.

'There is something I must explain,' she began. 'You may have noticed that I have not once mentioned your mother.' I nodded.

'Well,' she continued in a low voice. 'It is better that way. There is nothing to be gained in upsetting your grandmother. Incidentally that was why I discouraged her from speaking about the past, earlier on.' I replied that I had deduced as much.

'I know that you were not against dearest Mama,' I added, 'Papa told me so. He said you did your best for her...and for him.' The sallow face on a level with my own turned a dull red. I supposed my compliment had embarrassed her. At first she did not comment on what I had said, but after a moment looked at me thoughtfully and said:

'Seeing you brings it all back.' Then she brightened, called across to Lavinia to button-up well against the wind and announced that they really must be going.

She suggested that I stroll a little way up the drive with Lavinia.

'I will follow in a minute or two. Francis and I have business matters to discuss.'

I did as she requested and found Lavinia agreeable company. She professed herself delighted at my coming, especially she added, since her mother had told her that we were about the same age.

'Your Grandmother wishes Mama and me to accompany you to the town as soon as possible,' she went on, 'and I'm *so* looking forward to it. I just adore choosing new gowns and bonnets and everything.' Her excitement was infectious and I found myself warming to her friendliness.

'If it is agreeable to everyone, let us go one day this week,' I suggested. Lavinia clapped her hands with approval. I asked her to tell me about her life, how she occupied herself, etc., and was told that she spent much of her time embroidering, walking, and paying social calls with her mother.

'But I only left the young ladies' academy six months ago,' she continued, 'and as we began our travels in Europe soon after I came home, I have to date spent little time here. It will be all right in the summer, I expect, she said thoughtfully, 'but it may prove boring if we suffer some bad winters.' She withdrew her delicate little hands from the sable muff she wore and spread them dramatically. 'In a bad winter one can be confined to the house by snowfalls for days, which would be quite unsupportable.' She stopped, then whispered with an almost conspiratorial air:

'What I would truly like is to live in London, but Mama will not hear of it. It is almost as though she were chained to Gales Hill. Nothing will move her to live elsewhere, nothing. For myself I cannot see why she is so taken with the place.' She looked about her. 'It is too far from any town and there are so few people of our own class near at hand.'

'But what about the "prince-charming"?' I put in. She blushed.

'Oh,' she stamped her dainty foot, 'Mama is really *too* much sometimes... There is no one...at least...I cannot believe so. Oh I myself could swoon at his feet but he has said not a single word to give me hope...and oh, Helga, he is *so* handsome and debonair and I could die of love for him...And do you know,' she went on, dropping her voice to a whisper, 'I do believe he is quite, quite wicked too...he is the most daring and exciting man I have ever encountered...'

'Perhaps he will declare himself soon.'

'I pray so,' she replied fervently, her cheeks flushed, her eyes sparkling, 'otherwise I fear I cannot support the waiting.' Then with an abrupt change of mood she added morosely:

'But I am being fanciful, just like Mama. I do not think Mr. Southwold is interested in me at all.' Mr. Southwold! At the mention of his name, my heart lurched in an unaccountable manner. Pulling myself quickly together, I tried to console Lavinia.

'Your mother is a woman of the world,' I told her. 'She must have observed something in this gentleman's manner that prompts her hopes...Does...does he call upon you?'

'Twice,' she answered. 'He has called twice since I came home from the academy. It is not often.'

'But you have been away for some weeks, have you not?' I reminded her. 'Now that you are home again, perhaps Mr. Southwold will visit soon.'

'Perhaps,' she agreed, but with little conviction I thought. Poor child, she was of a certainty consumed with emotion of some kind, but whether of true love or infatuation I could not determine. I found it difficult to remember that we were nearly the same age, for in her child-like candour she seemed so much younger than myself. No doubt she had had a very sheltered life, I reflected, and in consequence was probably suggestible and vulnerable. Actually she was, in spite of her doll-like prettiness, the last person whom I would have expected Edward Southwold to court, and I thought that perhaps Grandmama had been correct in considering Mrs. Lewis over-presumptuous. It could have been a case of wishful thinking, I decided, recalling what Francis had told me earlier. We had reached the Dower House. I took my leave of Lavinia and made my way back. I had expected to meet Mrs. Lewis somewhere along the path, but there was no sign of her. Her talk with Francis must have taken longer than she anticipated. But when I entered the house there was no sign of either of them. I concluded that they must have left through one of the rear entrances. Before rejoining Grandmama, I ran upstairs to take off my cloak. As I walked along the landing I suddenly had the strangest feeling that I was not alone. I stopped and looked nervously about me down the long shadowy corridor. My own chamber was at the far end. Of the other doors, all except one were closed. I crept silently towards it and as I passed, glanced swiftly through the half-open doorway. In the room stood Mrs. Lewis. She was alone. She was standing perfectly still and had her back towards me. I thought she was staring at something on the far wall. She did not hear my steps and I did not disturb her. Feeling relieved that my nervousness had had no foundation I went on to my own chamber. No doubt Mrs. Lewis was about some household matter for my grandmother.

Later that night as I lay in bed going over the events of the day in my mind, two matters troubled me. One was my reaction to the news that Lavinia was in love with Edward Southwold. The other was the realisation that in spite of Mrs. Lewis's friendliness towards me, I did not like her.

I had a habit each night of writing in my journal. The first night at Gales Hill I had recorded my impressions, ending with the words: 'I do not hate my grandmother as much as I expected to do.' Getting out of bed I took my journal from the dressing-table drawer and added another sentence to that day's writings. It took the form of a question: 'Why do I dislike Mrs. Lewis?'

SIX

And so my days at Gales Hill began, days in which I strove, fairly successfully I believe, to establish a reasonably agreeable relationship with my grandmother.

It was not as difficult as I had initially imagined for we did not see such a great deal of each other in the course of a day and because of this there was less chance of discord between us. Grandmama, on account of her blindness, kept a great deal to her own rooms. There was a sitting-room leading off her bedchamber, and some days she took all her meals there, not coming downstairs at all. I saw her every day of course, visiting her in her rooms on those occasions when she elected to stay upstairs. Occasionally I would take her meals up to her and I made a point of sitting with her, either reading to her or conversing with her for at least some part of each day. She never mentioned my mother and if I myself made reference to her at all, she at once adroitly changed the subject. It irritated me but was perhaps the most sensible thing to do under the circumstances.

Francis sometimes came in to see her whilst I was there. He was always gay and charming in his manner towards her, with a great show of affectionate banter.

To be fair to him I believe he was fond of the old lady, but somehow I felt that his feelings were not all that deep. Amiable and pleasant though he was, I always sensed that he was rather shallow, incapable of deep commitment either to people or causes. But he was a likeable fellow, and apart from the odd fits of moodiness, congenial company. He rarely spent a full day at home. Where he went and what he did I had no idea. He rode off every morning, or nearly so, usually about noon. Sometimes he returned home for dinner, but on other nights he would be very late indeed. On one or two occasions when his coming up the stairs awakened me in the small hours, I suspected that he was the worse for strong drink. Certainly it was after such happenings that he slept especially late the next day. Whether Grandmama knew of his ways, I did not know, but once or twice she asked me if I had heard him come home the night before, so I think she suspected something.

Polly once told me that he gambled a lot.

'T'missus doesn't know,' she whispered. 'She'd 'ave a fit if she did, so don't let on, Miss, but he bets on the cocks.'

'The cocks?' I didn't understand what the girl was talking about.

''Aven't you never heard of cock-fighting?' she gasped. 'There's plenty of it going on. They arrange fights in t'malt kiln in the mill on a Sunday morning, Mr. Francis and the rest of 'em, while other folks is in t'church.'

'You mean they deliberately set the birds against each other?'

'Yes, of course. And the gents place bets about which of 'em's going to win. Our Billy goes sometimes and he says it isn't half exciting. They have spurs on their legs and go for one another like all that–'

'It sounds terrible,' I interrupted. 'Cruel.'

81

'That's what me mam says,' returned Polly. 'The first time she found out our Billy had sneaked in to watch she gave him a good skelping, but she can't now 'cos he's over big. Mind, Miss, I reckon it's t'barrel of ale they 'ave what attracts him as much as t'fight.' She went on to tell me, and I couldn't help but smile at the way she spoke, that the man who kept the cocks let them roost in his house.

'And you can bet what a mucky mess they make, can't you, Miss?' she concluded.

I did, naturally, respect Polly's confidence and divulged nothing of our conversation to Grandmother. Nor did I speak of it to Francis himself. It was none of my business. But I did wonder how much betting took place on these occasions and whether large sums of money were involved. I supposed it depended on the class of people who made up the spectators: if most of them were gentlemen like Francis it seemed likely that sizeable amounts might change hands. And I wondered if his bouts of moodiness were the result of spells of ill luck.

What his financial situation was I naturally did not know, but one could not fail to see how extravagant he was. One day he showed me his horses (he rode to hounds in the season), two splendid animals even to my unknowledgeable eyes. They must have cost a great deal of money. And his clothes, as I had noticed from the very first, were lavish in the extreme. Francis would take it hardly, I reflected, should he ever fall upon hard times.

But apart from that second day at Gales Hill when he had shown me round, I had seen little of him. In a sense he was a bit of a mystery to me. He never spoke of his friends, or brought any of them home with him. What Polly had told me of him earlier had suggested that he might be a philanderer and I wondered if I might have trouble with him, but his behaviour had been exemplary. To be honest I think he was quite indifferent towards me.

Mrs. Lewis and Lavinia I had seen a great deal, especially the former who visited us every day without fail. When I tentatively suggested that I might perhaps relieve her a little of the task of managing Grandmama's household, she wouldn't hear of such a notion.

'It is thoughtful of you to offer,' she told me, 'but there is absolutely no need at all for you to trouble yourself with these things. And without casting the smallest aspersions on your efficiency my dear, no one could manage better than I—it was my home.'

As time went by I was beginning to like her a little more but still with reservations. She was kindness itself to me and I chided myself at being over-sensitive and critical but sometimes could not rid myself of the suspicion that she was putting on an act, that in her heart of hearts she cared little for me.

For Lavinia my affection grew stronger with each passing day. There was a child-like directness about her which I found wholly pleasing, and she was so very pretty that she was an absolute joy to look upon. It surprised me that Francis did not seek her favour, but he seemed as indifferent towards her as he was towards me. Not that Lavinia would have welcomed his attentions with her heart so full of longing for Mr. Southwold.

Two or three days after my arrival, the poor girl had been stricken with a chill and had been confined to her room for several days. Because of this we had not, as yet, made our proposed visit to the shops in the local market town. I had visited her every day of her indisposition, an indisposition she suffered with great impatience.

'I am so wearied of this one room,' she wailed. 'How I should have endured it without you, Helga, I really cannot imagine. With no one but Mama for company I do not know how I could have supported the boredom of it.' When the initial fever had passed I suggested that the time might pass more quickly if she engaged herself upon her embroidery but she said she was sick to death of the sight of her sampler and hadn't the least intention of sewing another stitch for some time to come. When her condition improved sufficiently we occasionally took gentle walks together in the grounds, and her spirits began to improve.

One day when the sun shone quite warmly, we ventured farther afield and strolled along the lanes for a short while. We had walked a little way when a phaeton appeared round a bend in the road. In it was Edward Southwold. On reaching us he stopped and enquired courteously as to Lavinia's health: he had heard of her indisposition from one of his tenants whom he had been visiting. My arm through Lavinia's, I felt her tremble with excitement as she thanked him for his concern and replied that she was well on the way to recovery. She then at once introduced me:

'May I present Miss Helga Radford, Mr. Southwold. She has come to live with her grandmother at Gales Hill.' Edward Southwold acknowledged the introduction with a smile and bowed courteously in my direction. I in turn did likewise. I wondered if he would mention the fact that we had already met, but he did not do so. No doubt, I thought angrily, he would have ignored me again had not Lavinia's introduction made it impossible.

'Dear Helga has been such a comfort,' Lavinia chattered, 'I owe it entirely to her cheerful company that I have not become melancholy these last days.' I interjected that such an idea was nonsense: I had done nothing.

'I am sure it is far from being nonsense,' Edward Southwold said smiling, but with a sardonic gleam in his eyes. He turned back to Lavinia.

'I myself have enjoyed the benefit of Miss Radford's company. I know just how stimulating she can be.' Lavinia gaped. She turned towards me.

'You did not tell me you had met Mr. Southwold!'

'I was able to give Miss Radford a lift in my carriage on the night of her arrival here,' he explained to her before I could say a word. 'Our encounter was brief, but extremely interesting.'

I still smarted at his cursory treatment of me that day with Francis and I thought he was being sarcastic.

'Fancy keeping a thing like that to yourself!' Lavinia's eyes were wide. 'Why didn't you tell us Helga?'

Conscious of Edward Southwold's mocking gaze I replied lightly, 'It seemed too trivial a matter to be worthy of mention.'

I saw the keen grey eyes narrow slightly at my words and I fancied for a moment that some stinging rejoinder would be forthcoming. But to my surprise he did not retaliate. At once I regretted my rather waspish remark. What was the matter with me, I asked myself irritably, that I could not behave politely and rationally towards this man?

'Trivial?' Lavinia was incredulous. 'Trivial, that you had ridden with Mr. Southwold?'

Clearly amused at the girl's transparency he replied:

'It appears, Miss Lewis, that your friend was not impressed by the occasion.' Though his words were to Lavinia, he eyes were upon me. The mocking expression had gone, replaced by one that I could not fathom. For a split second it was almost as though we had both completely forgotten Lavinia's presence. Then trembling slightly before that deep, questing gaze, I looked quickly away.

'Isn't he just *too* handsome,' sighed Lavinia after he had taken leave of us. 'I almost swooned at the sight of him. How you could keep it to yourself that you had actually ridden in his carriage with him, I just cannot imagine. I would have told the world. It is what I *long* to do.' She gave a great sigh, her eyes still following the carriage till it disappeared from our sight. Only then did she turn towards me again.

'Why, Helga,' she cried, concern in her voice, 'how pale you have become. It is the sharp wind, I felt you shiver a moment or two ago. Come, let us return to the house.' I agreed without demur, relieved that she had divined nothing of my inner turmoil and was completely ignorant of the true cause of my pallor.

The moment we were back indoors, Lavinia told her mother of the meeting with Mr. Southwold.

'And what do you think, Mama, Helga has actually ridden in his carriage with him!' She went on to recount the full incident, much to my embarrassment. Watching Mrs. Lewis I could see that the initial satisfaction she had felt at her daughter's first piece of news was wiped out by the bit about myself. Try as she might, she was unable to hide her annoyance completely.

'Helga was quite right to regard the incident as being of no importance,' she announced when Lavinia had finally stopped chattering. 'After all, Mr. South-wold could hardly have acted otherwise in the circumstances...' She smiled as she spoke and there was logic in what she said, but the little barb behind her words did not escape me.

'Indeed,' I agreed, and the subject was dropped. Soon afterwards I left.

I was glad to be on my own again as it gave me a chance to try to sort out my feelings. Not only was I still a little disturbed by the encounter with Mr. Southwold, there was another matter on my mind that I wanted to think about. Something bothered me. It was a vague, nebulous sort of feeling that I had either seen or heard something, that morning or the day before, something important, but that I had failed to realise the implications of it. Frowning in concentration I carefully relived those last hours, but it was no use, I still could not bring whatever it was to mind. Thoroughly frustrated, I gave up. Perhaps it would come to me later, I decided, when I was not worrying over it.

During that night I suffered a bout of nausea. Pulling on my wrap I lit my candle and went downstairs to get a drink of water. It was two o'clock in the morning and I did not think I ought to wake any of the servants at such an hour. As I tip-toed back along the landing, anxious not to disturb the rest of the household, I suddenly noticed a light shining underneath one of the doors. I stopped in consternation. It was not the room that Francis had, nor was it Grandmother's. Very puzzled and a little nervous I put down my glass of water and knocked gently on the door. There was no response. I tried to turn the knob. But the door was locked. Then just as I was trying to decide what I ought to do about it, the light disappeared. Relieved, for the thought of a candle burning unattended (and the light had flickered as though from a candle) had worried me, I went back to my bed. I did not know what to make of the incident and in the end began to wonder if the moonlight had been playing tricks on me.

Next morning I questioned Polly. Had she, or any of the servants, left a light unattended in one of the bedchambers last night. The girl shook her head, obviously surprised by my question. After I had dressed I went back to the room in question. This time the door was open. I looked carefully around. It was a bedchamber but obviously unused. There was no sign of either a lamp or a candle. I smiled to myself. Truly I must have been a little confused last night, the sick headache had no doubt affected my vision. There had been no one, and no light other than the moon's.

It was only later, when I was taking my breakfast, that a question confronted me. If nobody had been there why had the door been locked? It was a question I could not answer. Because it was the same room that I had seen Mrs. Lewis in the day before, I mentioned the incident to her.

'Oh, that room,' she smiled. 'The door sticks. Your hands were full, you didn't try hard enough.'

A simple explanation which should have convinced me, but I had the strangest feeling that it wasn't the whole truth... However, as I never saw the light again I dismissed the matter from my mind.

And so the first weeks passed. At first the novelty of my new situation and the unaccustomed luxury of my surroundings kept me reasonably content. But soon they began to pall and I began to grow restless. In my soul I felt that I existed rather than lived in the true sense, and an odd sensation of unreality, of waiting for something to happen often came upon me. I was bored and I still felt like a stranger, that I did not belong...Strange though it may seem, it was only the brief encounters I had had with Edward Southwold that held any real meaning for me...

Once or twice I was tempted to forget my promise to Papa and go and seek my own way in the world. Perhaps it would have been better if I had. It would have saved me much anguish of heart and of mind...And yet, who knows? Who can be sure about these things? Now that it is all in the past I often wonder whether, even had I left, my ultimate destiny would have been the same...Is there indeed a divinity that shapes our ends...?

But I did not leave. I stayed. And the chain of events that constituted my fate, destiny, call it what you will, continued on its inexorable way...

SEVEN

I awoke one morning feeling especially depressed. The prospect of the aimless existence before me seemed more than usually appalling. Although they had been in abeyance for a while, I had not, contrary to Mama's and Papa's prophecy, 'grown out of' my 'unsuitable yearnings' and I knew that I could never be content with a life made up of such as I had experienced over the last few weeks. Nor, even had Mrs. Lewis allowed me to try, could I have entirely absorbed myself in domesticity. There had to be something more. In a way I envied those women, of whom Lavinia I believed was one, who sought nothing more from life than to fall in love, marry, and bring up a family. Could I have been this way, life would have been easier and much more comfortable. But I was powerless to change my nature, and I was pursued by impossible dreams and a compulsion to endeavour to make them a reality: what I, alone, could do to fight the cruelty, the injustice, the greed and pride in the world would be little indeed. Of that I was only too aware. It seemed a hopeless task. But I knew I had to try. Ever before me I kept an old Chinese proverb I had read somewhere, 'It is better to light one small candle than to curse the darkness.' I knew that if ever I was to have complete peace of mind, I must light that one small candle, however feeble and flickering its flame might be.

As I reflected upon these things, an idea came to me. I recalled what Francis had said about the farmhands of the area: how abysmally illiterate they were. So far I had had no contact with any of these unfortunates but I had observed them from time to time labouring in the fields around Gales Hill. They appeared to be just as Francis had described them, a shambling, slouching, boorish set of creatures, even to the sympathetic onlooker I felt myself to be. Perhaps with these people lay the opportunities for which I was searching. At once I felt excited. Thanks to Grandmama's allowance (which she had insisted was to begin at once) I now had money enough and to spare. I could easily afford to purchase books and slates and with their aid teach some of these poor Wolds people to read and write. It would provide me with a purpose in life.

I said nothing of all this, of course, to Grandmama, or to Francis. They would not have understood. And in any case I knew that I would have to tread warily, to be careful about presenting my ideas. For I had to face the possibility that the farmhands might scorn my endeavours: that they were probably content as they were with no desire to change or to widen their horizons. Far better, for the moment, I decided, to keep my intentions to myself, but at the same time to be alert to any opportunities.

The immediate problem facing me, however, was how to gain contact with the farming people. Francis had said it would be in order for me to visit the farms but I felt I could not present myself uninvited into their midst.

Grandmama, fortunately, provided me with an introduction. When I mentioned to her, after breakfast that morning, that I was desirous of looking over a Wolds farm and meeting the farming people, she seemed extremely pleased and at once suggested that I visit the farm nearest to Gales Hill.

'It is right and proper that as my granddaughter, you should show a certain care and interest towards the lower classes,' she announced. 'The Colmans are a worthy couple, good, sober, industrious people. They are well known to me and will feel honoured that you have condescended to visit them. Polly is their foreman's daughter. She can take you along.'

Without further preamble she pulled the bell-rope and when Polly appeared instructed the delighted girl to leave whatever she was about, put on her cloak and escort 'Miss Helga' to the Colman's farm.

It was a square house, not particularly attractive. The farm buildings stood in juxtaposition to it in a sort of quadrangle, with the foldyard in the centre, and a spacious stockyard with the cart, wagon, and implement sheds conveniently situated on one side of it. In front of the house was a small grass plot with a few flower beds and shrubs. It looked as though scant attention was paid to it. As with Gales Hill, narrow plantations of trees bounded the farmstead to the north and east. These belts of trees, I learned later, were intended not so much for ornament as for affording some protection from the biting northern and eastern blasts of winter and early spring. As we approached the farm I remembered that Francis had told me that Edward Southwold often visited his tenant farmers, the Colmans most of all. What if he were to visit them at the same time as myself, I mused. Oddly enough the possibility did not displease me...In spite of his mocking, his teasing and the slight insolence of that intent gaze I knew I enjoyed sparring with him...

I took to the Colmans on sight.

Especially Mrs. Colman. She was small, in sharp contrast to the bulk of the man who was her husband. Her slight frame heavy with the child she carried, she moved slowly and a little awkwardly. But for her eyes, her face, round and pale under tightly drawn-back hair, would have been plain. Her eyes more than redeemed it: huge and dark they shone with a goodness and gentleness such as I had seldom encountered. At first glance, when Polly had made the introductions I had thought her to be much younger than the man beside her, only a few years older than myself perhaps, but on looking more closely I saw that she was well into her middle years. There were streaks of grey in the thinning hair and tell-tale lines about her eyes and forehead. And in spite of the warm smile of welcome, she looked drawn and weary. An inexplicable surge of pity for her swept over me and with it a protective, almost maternal feeling, engendered perhaps by her smallness and frailty.

'Miss Helga wants to look round t'farm,' announced Polly. 'She's never been on one in all her life.' Then assuming the superior air of one in possession of facts unknown to her listeners, went on excitedly:

'She's lived in foreign parts, 'as Miss Helga...'

'Yes, Polly, so you told us earlier,' Mrs. Colman gently interrupted. 'Now off you go back to Gales Hill and your duties. Seth and I will escort Miss Radford home when she is ready.'

The girl did as she was bid, reluctantly, I felt, but without demur, for she had already been instructed by my grandmother to return immediately.

I spent a pleasant and interesting morning. Mr. Colman I found a little taciturn and abrupt at first but it occurred to me that his gaucheness of manner might be due to nervousness. He was not a man to converse easily with strangers. Only when he began to explain to me something of the nature of his farming did he lose his awkwardness and reserve. It was evident that his heart was very much in his work. His wife quickly became at ease with me and hardly ever stopped chattering.

The farm, I was told, was large, over six hundred acres in all, and required a goodly number of farmhands to work it. They all lived-in.

'Lived-in?' I did not quite understand.

Mrs. Colman looked surprised by my ignorance.

'They live in the farmhouse with us,' she explained. 'All except the foreman. He lives in the village, he's married. All the lads are single.'

I said that it must be a hard task feeding them all and looking after them but she replied that she had two 'good strong girls', who also lived-in, to help her.

We were just about to leave the huge farmhouse kitchen, a room gleaming with pewter and oak, when the door opened and a young man appeared. At sight of me he stopped, amazement covering his features. I guessed him to be about my own age, or perhaps a little younger. With his coming the atmosphere changed. I was aware of it instantly, a tension that had not been there previously.

There was no need to ask who the newcomer was for the wide brown eyes in the handsome young face were exactly those of his mother. He was slight of build, distressingly thin in truth, and only in his tallness did he at all resemble Mr. Colman. Mrs. Colman broke the silence that had fallen.

'This is Jason our son. Jason, this is Miss

Radford from Gales Hill.'

For a moment the young man remained just within the kitchen, almost as though incapable of movement, staring at me. Then suddenly he walked swiftly towards me and held out his hand. He seemed nervous and ill at ease, as awkward and self-conscious as his father. I smiled in as warm a fashion as I could in an effort to help him and was rewarded with a shy, almost timid smile, in return. His mother tried to draw him out, endeavouring to get him to engage in conversation with me. But he showed little response to her overtures and just stood there, silent, looking at me. His father he ignored completely. It was an uncomfortable situation. I murmured that it was time I took my leave of them, and Mrs. Colman, obviously relieved, led the way outdoors at once. As I followed in her wake I looked back at the young man. He was still staring. But not at me this time. He was staring at his retreating father. And there was hatred in his eyes. I glanced swiftly at his mother and as our eyes met I saw that she knew what I had witnessed. For a moment fear and desperation flickered in the great brown eyes, but quickly recovering she turned to her husband and put an affectionate hand on his arm.

'Come, Seth dear,' she said gently. 'Let us walk along the path a little way with Miss Radford.'

Conscious that I had unwittingly chosen to visit them at the time of some family quarrel or other, I told them that there was no need for anyone to accompany me, I should be perfectly all right on my own. The relief on their faces, particularly that of Mrs. Colman, showed me I had made a wise decision.

I reached Gales Hill to find an ornate chaise outside the front entrance and wondered idly whom it was who was calling on Grandmother. As I ran up the steps the door opened and out strode Edward Southwold. At sight of him my heart took an unaccountable leap. He smiled, bowed and held out his hand. As I placed my own within it a tremor shot through me. Quickly gaining control of myself I replied to his greeting, schooling my voice to a polite, formal tone. He had, he told me, called to pay his respects both to Grandmama and myself, and added that he hoped I was settling down happily in Yorkshire. I thanked him for his concern but gave a somewhat non-committal reply to his question.

'At first I found your county bleak, cold and harsh,' I told him. 'But now the place is beginning to grow on me if you know what I mean.'

'I do indeed,' he replied. Silence fell between us. I looked down at my feet, unable to think of anything further to say to him. I was conscious of his eyes upon me, but kept my gaze lowered. Within seconds he wished me good-day. Then just before he got into his carriage he turned and climbed back towards me.

'People can grow on one, too,' he announced softly to my great surprise. 'That is, provided they are given the opportunity. First impressions are rarely to be trusted.' Then, before I could gather my wits sufficiently together to answer him, he ran down the steps and was gone.

I did not go into the house immediately. I just stood there, motionless, on the top of the steps, watching the chaise and horses as they fairly flew down the drive. Then a smile slowly stealing over my features I turned and went inside. How amazing! Could it really be that the high and mighty arrogant English aristocrat had truly held out the olive branch? It would indeed appear so. The thought warmed my heart and a feeling of well-being came upon me.

At once a sense of shame smote me. There was treachery in such thoughts. This was the man whom little Lavinia avowed that she loved, and who, for all I knew, might love her in return. That my heart should be warming towards him spelt danger...I must keep a tight guard on my feelings before they gained a foothold. But then I decided that I was being ridiculous. Surely I could feel friendship towards the man. There was no wrong in that and that after all, was all I *did* feel towards him. Any other notion was too preposterous to be worthy of a single thought.

I did not feel like making conversation with Grandmama just then so I went straight up to my bedchamber. I took out my journal to write in something of the morning's events, and also to put within the pages a prettily shaped leaf that I had gathered on the journey home, to press it. There were two others already in the book, along with three flowers, five in all. I knew exactly where each one was. Opening the journal I put in my latest addition and turned the pages to inspect the others. To my surprise, one of them was missing. I searched in the drawer thinking it must have slipped from the pages. There was no sign of it. I returned to the journal and leafed through it. And there, three pages from where it should have been was the missing leaf. A little puzzled, I put it back to its appointed place and closed the book. Why had I moved the leaf, I wondered, and how was it that I had forgotten doing so?

EIGHT

I fully intended to visit the Colmans' farm again the very next day but as things turned out I was unable to do so. Mrs. Lewis came to see me early after breakfast and suggested that as Lavinia had now fully recovered we should all visit the nearby town so that I could purchase my new apparel. I agreed readily and so shortly after ten we set off in my grandmother's carriage. The outing proved to be pleasant and successful and I found my two companions interesting company, Mrs. Lewis especially. She obviously had a thorough knowledge of the town's history and pointed out several features that were of special interest. I caught my breath in surprise and delight at the first glimpse of it, an old red-roofed town lying at the foot of an incline. The roadway ran between wide green pastures which lay undulating like a sea as far as the eye could follow them. And down below, rising up clear and sharp were the slender towers of a fine cathedral.

'That is the Minster,' Mrs. Lewis informed me. 'In the old days many pilgrims journeyed here.' We entered the town beneath an old red gateway which admitted us to a wide street which in turn led to the market place. On the left of the street stood another fine church.

'This was once a place of refuge,' I was told as we passed by. 'Offenders of all kinds were granted sanctuary within its walls.' Then she went on to tell me that the old town had been a great meeting place for minstrels during medieval times.

'They came from all over the north on Rogation days to make music together with their rebecks.'

'Rebecks?' I questioned. It was a word I was unfamiliar with.

'A kind of fiddle,' she explained. 'It had only three strings, I believe.' Obviously Mrs. Lewis was a well-informed person. Lavinia took no part in this discussion at all. She seemed bored by it in fact. But when we reached the shops she was all animation and enthusiasm.

It was clear that neither the architectural beauty of the many fine buildings around us, nor the history of the place, had the least interest for her. When it came to choosing my clothes, however, she was of the greatest helpfulness, seemingly knowing at a glance which styles and colours would suit me the best. She bought one or two gowns for herself avowing she could not resist them, and a blue velvet bonnet in which she looked quite exquisite. And on the way home she chattered like an excited child about her purchases. For my own part I was quiet on the return journey. I was tired for one thing and also I had something on my mind.

It was the matter of my journal. For the more I thought about it, the more convinced I became that someone had been reading it. It came to me suddenly that not only had the pressed leaf been in the wrong place, the book itself had been too. I was almost completely certain that I had left it at the opposite end of the drawer than the one where I found it. The implications of such a conclusion were not agreeable to contemplate. Who in the household would stoop so low as to read such a private book? Grandmama was blind, and in any case was above such behaviour I was certain. Francis? A gay young blade such as he would have much more interesting ways in which to spend his time. It must have been Polly, I decided, or one of the other servants. Polly most likely, curious about somebody who was 'half-foreign' no doubt. It seemed the only explanation. Nothing really to worry about, I told myself, but a trifle unpleasant. If it happened again—or at least if I gained knowledge of its having happened again, I would have to question the girl, however distasteful such a task would be.

We were nearing the end of our journey, passing through the village which lay nearest to Gales Hill. Suddenly the carriage began slowing down and we heard sounds of a commotion coming from the roadway in front of us. Peering through the windows a strange sight met my eyes, a sight which both angered and revolted me. It was some sort of a funeral procession but the like of which I had never before witnessed and that I hope to God I never do again. Mrs. Lewis explained the situation. She seemed unmoved by it and I assumed that it must be commonplace.

'It's only a pauper who is being buried,' she told me, 'judging by the sweep's cart and the lack of pall-bearers and mutes.'

'But the boy,' I cried out, 'the boy clinging to the cart and making those horrible noises?' She looked again more carefully.

'Oh, that is the son. He's an idiot. It must be Mrs. Brown who is being put away. The boy obviously knows his mother is in the coffin. He must have seen her there before the parish women got her covered up with sawdust.'

She went on to explain that as the woman was a pauper she would be buried in the common burial ground at the expense of the parish, a wet, boggy piece of ground. The boy was still clinging on to the cart as we watched it turn towards the churchyard. Every now and then he would lay his head on the coffin and make a howling kind of groan which sounded like mam, mam, mamma. He was the only mourner. It was horrible to witness.

'What will become of him?'

'Oh, he'll be taken to the workhouse, unless there are relations or friends prepared to have him.' Mrs. Lewis was clearly unconcerned. I shuddered.

'How dreadful.' My companion shrugged and looked at me with some surprise.

'I suppose so,' she admitted. 'But there is nothing to be done about such things. God has ordained to each of us our position in life. The poor have to learn to be content in their low estate just as we are in our higher one. It is not for us to interfere. All we can do is to show charity to those of the poor who are deserving of it.'

It was an argument that I had heard many times before, an argument I could not accept.

'I am not at all sure that God *did* ordain such things,' I announced. 'It seems to me that many people are poor because of the greed of others and—'

'Oh, Helga, *do* stop talking about such boring matters.' It was Lavinia who broke in. 'You are becoming tedious I fear. And anyway, what can we women know of such things? It is better to leave everything to the gentlemen.'

'Of course it is.' Mrs. Lewis positively beamed on her daughter. 'Very well spoken, Lavinia dear. You show much good sense in your opinion. Such an attitude will prove to be a great asset to you in the future. Dear Mr. Southwold would wholly approve of your sentiments, I am sure.' She addressed herself to me once more: 'If I might offer a word of motherly advice, my dear, beware of appearing too clever. I know you are very beautiful to look upon, but believe me, it is unwise to talk like a blue-stocking, the gentlemen do not like it.'

I was prevented from replying to her little speech by the fact that we had arrived at Gales Hill.

'Ah, home at last,' Mrs. Lewis announced. 'Come along children, out you get. We should be just in time for tea.'

When Lavinia and her mother had left us, and I was alone with Grandmama, I told her about the idiot boy and how appalled I had been at the scene we had witnessed. I asked if there were no alternative for the poor wretch than the workhouse. She shook her head.

'None. Except of course, to become a beggar. The boy is fortunate in living in the country. For many town children the street is the only choice.'

'What is it like in an English workhouse, Grandmama?' I questioned. 'Will the boy be kindly treated?'

'He will have a roof over his head and food to eat,' she replied. 'And can expect nothing more.'

'But no one will really care about him, will they?' I began, and was suddenly seized with a wild, impossible idea. 'Could he come here to live, Grandmama? If no one else will have him, I mean.'

'Here? Indeed not. You must have taken leave of your senses ever to entertain such a notion.'

'But there is room,' I urged. 'The attics are all empty. I saw them when Francis showed me round. He could sleep there. And cook and the maids seem such kindly people they would not mind him in the kitchen. Oh please say yes, Grandmama.' I ran across the room and dropping down on the rug before her chair took her hands between my own in my entreaty. 'Please do say yes.'

She did not reply at once and her hesitation gave me hope. I thought it was a sign that she was weakening. And I was right.

'The idea is utterly ridiculous,' she began 'But on the other hand, I suppose it could do no harm—' I threw my arms round her neck.

'Oh, thank you Grandmama. You will not regret your goodness of heart, I assure you. The boy can be taught to be useful. He can learn to gather wood for the fires and to help in the garden, and perform all manner of simple errands.'

'Perhaps,' she replied wryly. 'On the other hand he may turn out to be completely impossible and without any sense in his poor addled head at all—in which case,' she added grimly, 'he will have to be sent either to a lunatic asylum or back to the workhouse, you understand?' Her words sobered me a little. It had never occurred to me that the boy might be uncontrollable.

'On reflection,' she went on, 'it would be advisable to consult someone else first, the vicar or Mr. Southwold. Both are Poor Law Guardians, I know. They may know about the boy's condition and the extent

113

of his affliction.' It was, of course, a sensible suggestion and one that I could not possibly disagree with.

'How soon can we talk with them, Grandmama?' She shook her head in mock dismay.

'What an impatient girl you are! But then I suppose if we are to proceed with your madcap idea at all we may as well get on with it. I will have messages sent to the Hall and the Vicarage early tomorrow morning.'

'And you will ask both gentlemen to come at once?' A glimmer of a smile played about her lips.

'You have much to learn, my dear child. In polite society we do not summon. I shall write and ask Mr. Southwold and the vicar if they will please call upon us at their convenience.'

'Well I hope they come soon,' I returned.

As things turned out, they both arrived the very next afternoon. Each in turn had sent a message accepting the invitation to call forthwith. Both had stated around three o'clock as being the time of arrival.

I dressed especially carefully that day, putting on the most attractive of my new gowns. It was a day dress of blue silk which Lavinia had said became me well and I believed, modestly I hoped, that such was indeed the case. The colour certainly matched my eyes. Unaccountably nervous, for I was not of a nervous disposition as a rule, I sat with Grandmother in the drawing-room, waiting for three o'clock to arrive. By the time Polly finally ushered the visitors in I was in a state of agitation. I told myself that it was because I was anxious as to the outcome of the proposed suggestion, and nothing more. Even to myself I was unwilling to admit that the greatest cause of my confusion was the prospect of being in Edward Southwold's company again.

I felt myself shiver with nervousness the moment he entered the room. His presence seemed to fill the place, to dominate, and I found myself having to drag my attention away from him and reply to the vicar's greetings. It was, of course, my first meeting with the Reverend Sykes. I remembered what Emma had said concerning his liberal ideas and felt at once a certain affinity with him. He was young, about thirty I supposed, and personable to look upon being of goodly height and pleasant of feature. But at the side of Edward Southwold he was colourless, I reflected. My reaction irritated me beyond words. Comparisons were odious at any time, I chided myself. The vicar was no doubt a man of personality and learning, equal probably, in every way, to his companion. I must not allow Mr. Southwold's magnetism to rob me of my powers of judgement, I told myself. Oddly ill at ease and absurdly tongue-tied, I sat mute, while my grandmother informed the two gentlemen of what I had suggested, and sought their advice.

Mr. Sykes was enthusiastic from the first. As far as he knew there were no relatives to take the poor lad, he informed us. 'And it would be an act of tremendous charity on your part to take him in, Mrs. Radford,' he went on. 'He is simple, of course, with only a modicum of intelligence, but docile, and quite manageable.'

'And what is your opinion, Mr. Southwold?' It was Grandmother who asked the question.

'I know little about him, I'm afraid,' came the reply. 'He and his mother lived in one of my cottages but beyond seeing the boy in the village street I have no knowledge of him. My steward would have more to tell you on the matter. However, from what our friend here says, there is surely no need to seek further information. It is a very worthy sentiment on the part of Miss Radford—and yourself, of course, and I applaud such a charitable spirit.'

Such totally unexpected praise and support made me blush furiously and a delicious feeling of joy flooded my being. I don't know why, but I had half expected him to oppose me, out of a sheer devilment of which I felt certain he was capable when it suited him, and so his support and enthusiasm came as a wonderful surprise.

I thanked him warmly, colouring again in my happiness and confusion. It was agreed to leave all the arrangements to the two gentlemen. Tea was brought in and conversation drifted to other matters. The vicar, talking with me alone while Mr. Southwold conversed with Grandmama, asked concerning my father. My surprise must have shown on my face. He explained that it was he who had read my father's letter to Grandmama.

'Francis was away from home when it came. I happened to call that morning and when the maid brought it in your grandmother asked me to open and read it to her.' He patted my arm in a fatherly way. 'So I do understand a little of your circumstances,' he said softly. 'No details, of course, but sufficient to realise that there was a family quarrel in the past. And if I may say so, it gladdens my heart to see that the rift is being healed somewhat. Family disputes can have grievous consequences at times.'

'Indeed they can,' I agreed. 'They are perhaps the saddest of all happenings. It is strange, is it not, how people who love one another can inflict such hurt upon each other. One cannot wonder at wars when people of the same flesh and blood cannot live in peace together.'

'If I may say so,' replied Mr. Sykes, 'you show wisdom beyond your years, Miss Radford.' There was no mistaking the sincerity of his tone. 'It is a pleasure to converse with a young lady of such perception and intelligence.' I felt tremendously pleased at the compliment and I wished, unworthy though such a wish no doubt was, that Mrs. Lewis could have heard it. She was in error in her assumption that all gentlemen disapproved of women discussing matters of moment. At this juncture Mr. Southwold strolled across the room towards us and asked me how I had enjoyed my visit to the Colmans' farm. I replied that I had found it immensely interesting and hoped to go again very soon.

'Perhaps you would care to see more of my estate?' My heart leapt.

'Indeed yes,' I replied promptly. 'I am anxious to learn as much as I can about the people of the area and the way in which they live.'

'Then I will escort you round—next week sometime, perhaps?' I told him that any day the next week would suit me admirably and that I should greatly look forward to the outing.

We were in the entrance hall and the two gentlemen taking their leave of us when Mrs. Lewis and Lavinia walked in. Their delight on encountering Mr. Southwold was revealingly obvious. I got the feeling that the gentleman himself found it slightly amusing. He replied to their effusive greetings with courtesy and charm but something, some shade or nuance of tone perhaps, made me doubt his sincerity.

'Please do not go on our account,' Mrs. Lewis begged. 'Lavinia and I can visit some other time; it is, after all, our second home here.'

Edward Southwold smiled down at her and answered her that both he and the vicar had been on the point of departing even before the two ladies arrived.

'I should feel so distressed,' Mrs. Lewis continued, 'if I felt we had driven you away—'

'Believe me, dear lady,' he interrupted, 'no one drives *me* away before I am ready to leave, not on any occasion, I assure you.' He turned towards me and held out his hand.

'Goodbye, Miss Radford. Shall we say today week for the tour of the estate?'

'Tour of the estate?' echoed Mrs. Lewis, a sharp tone in her voice. Mr. Southwold explained. At once she was all smiles again.

'What a splendid idea. It encourages the lower classes if we more fortunate beings show an interest in them. Perhaps you would like Lavinia to accompany you my dear?' She turned towards her daughter who, standing a little behind her, nodded ecstatically. I replied that of course I would be delighted for Lavinia to come along. Mrs. Lewis turned back to Mr. Southwold.

'I do hope my suggestion is not out of order,' she gushed, 'but dear Lavinia is much too retiring and ladylike to suggest such a thing herself, and I know Helga would wish for her company: the two have become *such* friends. They took to each other from the very first moment...' She stopped, smiling from one to the other of us before continuing: 'Even though they are so different in almost every way...' I saw the way Edward Southwold's eyes narrowed slightly at her little speech and wondered what he made of it. Giving nothing away, however, he replied urbanely:

'There is no need to apologise, Mrs. Lewis. It is a first-rate notion. And I am sure my steward will be delighted to have the company of your charming daughter as well as that of Miss Radford.'

Mrs. Lewis's face fell. Lavinia's too. Their dismay was so obvious as to be almost comical. The mother quickly recovered.

'Then it is settled. Thank you, Mr. Southwold.' She smiled. Lavinia was not as adept at concealing her feelings.

'Let us hope it is a warm, calm day,' she pouted. 'You know how I hate the cold, Mama, and the howling winds with dust blowing on one's shoes and gown, and how soon I take a chill—'

'That is a point to be borne in mind,' her mother interrupted her. 'And sensible of you to bring it up, Lavinia dear, just in case we have to give backword.' She smiled up at Edward Southwold again: 'Such a considerate daughter,' she confided. 'No woman could wish for a better one. Lavinia is careful of her health solely because she knows how worried I become if she is indisposed in the slightest degree.'

'Then you are indeed fortunate, Ma'am,' murmured Mr. Southwold. 'And please do not give the matter another thought.' He turned towards me:

'If Miss Lavinia is unable to accompany you, Miss Radford, I'm sure you will understand perfectly.' I inclined my head, a glow of happiness suffusing my being. For that one swift glance, that one sentence had established a bond between us. He had seen through Mrs. Lewis's rigmarole and he knew that I also had done so. He had paid me the compliment of assuming my intelligence equal to his own. I hugged the thought to myself, treasuring it. This was what I had wanted, that he should respect me for myself, not just for my family name as had seemed on that first meeting. And suddenly in a blinding flash of self-revelation I knew why, right from the start it had been so important to me that this should be so. I was in love with him! And I had been, although I had not realised the fact, probably from the very first moment. That was why his seeming indifference had piqued me so: because I had never for one moment, been indifferent towards *him*. And even when I had tried to convince myself that what I wished for was only friendship towards him, deep down in my heart I must have known it was not the truth. Like my dear mother before me I had fallen wildly, deeply in love at first sight and nothing could alter the fact. Lest my eyes betray the intensity of my feelings I swiftly lowered my gaze.

Outwardly composed I bid him good-day, took leave of the Reverend Sykes, and accompanied Mrs. Lewis and Lavinia back to the drawing-room. They did not stay long and I was pretty certain in my own mind that the sole purpose of their visit had in truth been to see Mr. Southwold. No doubt they had seen the carriage coming up the drive. Mrs. Lewis would not be likely to miss any opportunity of throwing Lavinia and him together. Poor little Lavinia. My heart ached for her, for I knew now with sure certainty that Edward Southwold did not favour her at all. In an inexplicable way I knew that even though he were never to fall in love with me, he would never love her. I hoped most sincerely that her feelings for him were not as deep as she imagined. If so, much heartache lay in store for her. That he was aware of her devotion, perhaps even amused by it, there was little doubt. He probably considered it to be no more than a schoolgirl infatuation that she would out-grow but I prayed that he would, gently and soon, let her see that he did not return her feelings. And I vowed, then and there, that as long as Lavinia nursed any hope of winning his love, I myself would never reveal, by so much as one word or look, how I felt towards him.

I nursed a certain anger and impatience with Lavinia's mother in having raised the poor girl's hopes. No doubt she meant well and was, like most parents, anxious for her daughter to make a good match, but to raise hopes on so slender a foundation as Lavinia had revealed to me, was both cruel and futile. What a blessing it would be, I mused, if Lavinia were to fall madly in love with someone else. I hoped with all my heart that she would...and soon...

That night, as usual, I took out my journal to write of the day's happenings. I was careful this time to record nothing of my feelings. I kept them locked safely away in my heart. In a sense, I was happier that night than I had ever been in my life before. In spite of the uncertainty of the future, for I had no guarantee that my love for Edward Southwold would ever be reciprocated, I felt like a new being. I was alive as opposed to existing, with a new awareness of all around me. It was a moonlit night, a night of many stars and I stood at my window and gazed out over the sweeping wolds. I had done the same thing before and been unmoved by the scene. But tonight I saw through new eyes, the eyes of love. What before had seemed ordinary, appeared to me now as of incomparable beauty. How blessed it is to love... more wonderful perhaps than *being* loved...

That night I stood on the mountain tops. I got into bed and lay savouring my new-found happiness and going over the day's events in my mind. Thinking over the conversation with the vicar I suddenly began to feel puzzled about something. Why, I wondered, had Grandmama asked *him* to open and read her letters to her? Why had she not left them until Francis came back? He had only been absent from Gales Hill for the one day. It seemed strange, I thought, not to have waited for him...

NINE

It was one week later, the day I was to make a tour of the estate with Mr. Southwold's steward. As I dressed, I felt a pleasurable anticipation of the outing, tinged, naturally, with regret that it was not to be Edward himself, as I now shyly sometimes thought of him, who was to accompany me.

As I had fully expected to happen, a message came from the Dower House that

Lavinia would not be joining me: she was a little indisposed, her note revealed, and as the wind was cold, she deemed it advisable to remain indoors. I could not help smiling to myself as I read the letter. Had Edward been the one to show us around, not even the most biting blast would have prevented her from joining us, of that I felt sure.

At ten-thirty the gig from the Hall arrived, and to my amazement and joy it was Mr. Southwold himself who was driving it. His steward, he said, was engaged on other duties that morning, and so he himself had elected to show me his estate. Wildly happy and excited I thanked him warmly for his consideration. As the gig was open, I was glad of my new woollen morning gown and cape which were thick and warm. I wondered whether Mr. Southwold would comment on Lavinia's absence but he did not do so: like me, no doubt, he had anticipated it. As I thought on such lines a sudden, wonderful idea came to me. Had he, I wondered, intended all along to show me round himself and had mentioned the steward's accompanying me alone to dissuade Lavinia from joining us? Oh, if only I could believe that it was so! It would mean that at least he felt a desire for my company in preference to hers. Then I chided myself at my wishful thinking. The idea was nonsense. He had come out of politeness, that was all, not wishing to upset my arrangements for the day.

I found him to be, as indeed I knew I should, a stimulating companion, and we discussed many interesting topics as we drove along. But first he enquired about the idiot boy who had been brought to Gales Hill three days earlier.

'Oh, he has settled down remarkably well,' I was happy to be able to tell him. 'Cook and the maids have been simply splendid with him and he has responded to their kindness in a manner beyond my fondest hopes.' And I went on to tell him how useful the boy was already becoming about the place. 'He chops wood for the fires, carries water, sweeps the courtyard and generally helps in all sorts of ways.'

'He is a fortunate young man,' Mr. Southwold commented 'to have attracted the attention of anyone so charitable as yourself. For most such creatures it is a vastly different story.' I could tell by the seriousness of his tone that he really did care about the conditions of the poor and it gave me the courage to tell him what I had in mind regarding the farmworkers. He listened attentively to what I had to say and to my joy, wholeheartedly supported the idea. He warned me, however, that I should tread warily.

'Not everyone, regrettably, shows your enlightened outlook on life, my dear Miss Radford. You will meet with opposition from some of the farmers, of that you can be sure. However,' he continued, 'as they are all my tenants, their opposition will become minimal if you let them know that your endeavours have my full approval.' He smiled at me so warmly as he gave me this encouragement that my heart almost turned over. Eyes shining, I thanked him for his readiness to help.

'There is no need of thanks,' he told me. 'Just to look at your face, so radiant with happiness, is all the reward I, or any man, could possibly wish for.' It was a most charming compliment and I found myself blushing furiously. Quickly I turned my head lest he read in my face how much his words had meant to me. Assuming a business-like approach, I told him that I hoped to begin my work with the farmhands at Colman's farm.

'I have visited the family several times now,' I explained, 'and have become quite attached to them. I feel sure that they will not object to my ideas. Mrs. Colman,' I continued, 'seems quite a cultured person—'

'I believe my steward told me once that her father was a minister of religion,' Mr. Southwold interrupted me. 'Which would perhaps account for it.'

'Possibly,' I agreed. We had turned in at the farm gates of the first tenants we were to visit, and the subject was dropped.

In the course of the day I was shown many farms, and learned much about the way of life of the wold farmers. One of the first things that I noticed was that at the entrance of almost every farmyard there was a circular pond where ducks and geeese were disporting themselves. Mr. Southwold explained that these ponds were artificial and had been carefully lined with clay to prevent the water running away through the porous chalk of which the Wolds are formed. They were also to be found here and there in outlying fields, he went on, and unless a summer was exceptionally long and dry, could be relied upon to supply water for the whole year for the horses and beasts.

'There is a dearth of rivers, springs and natural pools here,' he continued, 'and it is due to the fact that the chalk subsoil extends to a great depth, and water "sipes" away in underground currents. It does not appear again until it meets the clay at the boundaries of the district where it springs up in places—sometimes in great abundance.' He added that in wet seasons springs called 'gipses' gushed out at certain points with great force, creating strong rushing streams in some of the valleys.

'My steward, Hayward, tells me there are superstitions surrounding such waters,' he smiled. 'But no doubt it is all a lot of nonsense.'

On one farm that we visited I was shown the soot chamber. Mr. Southwold asked the farmer to tell me about it and I learned it was where the farmhands slept while on the job of spreading soot on the fields. It was a veritable black hole, in the farm buildings. There were heaps of straw for the men to lie on, and horsecloths and sacks with which to cover themselves. It appeared that during the operation they never doffed their sooty clothes from beginning to end.

'They're as black as Hottentots by t'time they've finished,' he went on in his broad Yorkshire dialect, and recounted how they needed to enlist the help of the servant girls in order to become clean again. Apparently a huge scalding tub was brought out and the men plunged into it one by one. The maids, armed with stiff scrubbing brushes and other cleansing materials laid about them with all the force at their command.

'The lads look forward to it,' he concluded. 'They 'ave a right merry time, I can tell you.' I was beginning to feel a little embarrassed at the tone the account had taken and cut him short before he could enlarge upon it. Mr. Southwold, I could see, was highly amused by the old man's tale but on sensing my confusion, quickly brought the interview to a close. I was grateful to him.

On the way home I asked about the terms of employment of the farm labourers. I learned that they were almost always engaged for service for a year and that the hiring took place at Martinmas in the latter half of November. These Martinmas hirings, fairings as they were often called, were held in all the market towns throughout the Riding. Seeing a likely looking lad, the farmer would approach him with a view to engaging him, asking questions about his capabilities, his last place and so on. If the answers pleased him, he would touch the important question of wage, and when terms were finally agreed, the farmer would give the servant his "fest" or godspenny, which might be a shilling or half a crown or so. This sealed the transaction and made the bargain legally binding on both sides.

'The hiring fairs are the highlight of the labourer's year,' Mr. Southwold went on. 'They are very jolly, boisterous affairs with merry-go-rounds, stalls and shows of all kinds much in evidence, and the labourers, of both sexes, decked out in their Sunday best. Martinmas week is, of course, the only real holiday they get.'

'I have heard that the farmhands, on the whole, are quite Godless. Is this true, do you suppose, Mr. Southwold?'

'I imagine so,' he replied. 'And the reason for it is not hard to find, I think. They lead, on the whole, isolated lives; they work from morn till night and retire to rest early. It is difficult for the clergy to get in touch with them. Many of the farms, as you have seen for yourself, are far away from any village.' I murmured that it was indeed a difficult situation.

'The greatest hindrance to gaining any influence over them,' he went on, 'is, the vicar tells me, the fact that they are only hired for a twelvemonth. For even if, by some fortunate chance, a lad does come under his teaching, at the end of the year he invariably moves on to some other farm, perhaps in a distant parish, and is seen no more.'

'It must be very frustrating,' I remarked.

'The clergy do their best, I am sure,' Mr. Southwold replied, 'but as you can see, there are many obstacles in their path. Very rarely do the lads enter any church, for if they did, being unable to read, they would feel out of their element.'

'But they could listen, Mr. Southwold.'

He smiled.

'It is evident that you have not yet made the acquaintance of our labourers. To most of them, illiterate as they are, the language of the Prayer Book would be almost like a foreign language.'

What he said quite appalled me and added to my determination to try to help these poor unfortunate yokels. If I succeeded in teaching only a handful of them to read, I should I felt, have dispelled a little of their darkness.

The outing was drawing to a close. As the horses turned into the lane leading back to Gales Hill my spirits fell. I could not remember anything that I had enjoyed so much. I knew of course, that it was not so much what I had seen and done that had been responsible for my happiness but rather the fact of with whom I had enjoyed these things. All day I had been conscious of a desire to please me, on Mr. Southwold's part. He had gone out of his way to show me everything I wished to see and to explain those in which I showed the slightest interest. We had discussed matters in detail and in depth, and throughout I had been treated as his absolute equal, both socially and intellectually. And not only that. To my joy I felt that I was being courted. Perhaps it was wishful thinking on my part, but in truth I do not believe so. His attitude to me was far warmer than mere courtesy demanded.

When we parted he held my hand and asked softly if he might call on me again in the very near future. Yes, cried my heart, Yes, Yes, Yes, come soon, tomorrow and everyday, whenever you wish! But in time I remembered Lavinia. Stifling my emotions, I replied evenly, coolly, that of course he could call, whenever he chose, Grandmama and I were always happy to receive him. It was not the response he had expected and I sensed the rebuff it gave him. A puzzled frown creased his forehead and a hard look chased the smile from his mouth and eyes. He withdrew his hand, bowed formally, murmured that he was always at my service and left.

Outwardly composed, weeping in my heart, I watched him drive away. In that moment I felt I hated Lavinia. But for her I could have let him see what he meant to me: that to be courted, wooed by him was what I longed for more than anything else in the world...Then I chided myself for being so ready to indulge in self-pity and reminded myself that no doubt what little Lavinia wanted more than anything in the world was also to be wooed by Mr. Southwold. And perhaps she *had* received encouragement to do so. The man was a charmer, skilled in words and manner in his dealings with women. A man, no doubt, of vast experience in such wiles...

I loved him, true, but casting aside the

matter of Lavinia, was he a person to be trusted? Assuming he was beginning to feel something for me, how did I know that his intentions were honourable?...The hot colour sprang to my cheeks as I recalled the bold, insolent look he had given me that first night. Was it feasible that he could have changed his attitude so quickly, I asked myself? Could it be that he played some game with me, a game already played with Lavinia and others...? Feeling confused and thoroughly wretched, I made my way slowly indoors.

'Still upon your feet?' I turned quickly as the laughing voice of Francis accosted me.

'Of course I am,' I snapped. 'Don't be ridiculous.'

'Ha, ha,' he returned. 'So you are not impervious to our Lord of the Manor's charm, after all, it seems.' At once I regretted my impetuosity. Francis was more perceptive than I had given him credit for.

'I'm sorry,' I apologised. 'I did not mean to speak so sharply. It is just that I am rather weary.'

'I understand,' he replied lightly. 'Forget it.' Looking into his face I knew that he did understand, and a great deal more than I wished him to at that. The incident upset me a little but served to put me fully on my guard against betraying my real feelings again either to Francis or anyone else.

For the rest of the day I was restless, unable to interest myself in anything properly, or apply myself to any task with dedication or concentration. After dinner I decided to go for a stroll in the grounds. It was a fairly dark night but the wind had dropped bringing a slight rise of temperature. Grandmama and I had dined alone as Francis was visiting friends somewhere in the locality.

It was when I was passing close by the gardens of the Dower House that I heard voices. I did not mean to eavesdrop, but on such a still night sound carried clearly and I could not help but overhear what was being said.

'You are sure of this?' It was Francis who spoke. I recognised his voice at once, much to my amazement. For when he had spoken of visiting friends I had never for one moment imagined he meant the Lewis's.

'Absolutely,' came the reply and it was Mrs. Lewis who made it. 'I was there,

It's all settled. But do not despair,' she continued. 'A lot may happen before...' I passed out of earshot and heard no more. What I had heard made little sense to me and I thought no more about it. I was too wrapped up in my own black mood to dwell very much on other people's problems. It was only later, much later in fact that subsequent events caused me to wonder about it...

On my next visit to the Colmans' farm I became acquainted with the farmhands. I had gone deliberately, at Mrs. Colman's suggestion, in the early evening when the day's work was finished. After they had partaken of their tea which they ate at a long scrubbed wooden table in the kitchen, Mrs. Colman introduced me to them. She had previously, at my suggestion, questioned them as to their desire to be taught to read and write at my hands, and to my gratification eight out of the ten of them had expressed themselves willing. I had gone armed with slates, books and pencils, and amid much nudging, giggling and gaping, the lessons began. Apart from one boy who seemed unusually bright, progress that first evening was almost nil. The main obstacle was a lack of understanding between us. My speech was as much a foreign tongue to them as theirs was to me. I could see that it was going to be a long, uphill struggle. Nevertheless I did not despair and by the end of the lesson we were at least able to communicate a little.

And so the routine of the lessons began and I felt I was making some contribution to life that was worthwhile. The first thing I tried to teach these young men was the catechism and some simple passages from the Bible, for it seemed to me that if I could instil some Christian truth into their minds and hearts my work would not be in vain.

During this time I saw nothing of Mr. Southwold and whether he knew of my work with the farmhands or not, I did not know. Francis expressed himself highly amused at my efforts while Grandmama, though tolerant about it on the whole, made it clear that in her opinion it was undesirable to give people ideas 'above their station' in life, and warned me against doing so. To Lavinia and her mother my behaviour was incomprehensible.

'How can you bear to waste time on such

clods, I really cannot imagine. To sit in the same room as them would be insufferable to me,' Mrs. Lewis announced. 'But of course,' she continued, smiling affably, 'everyone must behave according to their own dictates, and I suppose the matters are determined largely by background and upbringing—and of course, your mother was once only—' she stopped abruptly, a look of embarrassment covering her face.

'Only a governess,' I supplied lightly, hiding my anger. I did not intend to let her see that she had annoyed me but she was not easily deceived.

'Oh, Helga,' she cried with seeming remorse, 'please do not take offence. I meant no slight towards your mother. Teaching is a worthy profession and one to be respected.' Smothering my anger I accepted her explanation and tried to convince myself that it was genuine and sincere. I reminded myself how Papa had told me of her charitable attitude towards my mother. I was being ultra-sensitive. After all there was no gain-saying the fact that Mama *had* been a governess which was all that Mrs. Lewis had said.

But in spite of such arguments my initial reaction did not wholly disappear. Papa had had a very unsuspecting nature...he could easily have been deceived...Then I told myself I was being thoroughly stupid. Why should Mrs. Lewis, Emma, as she was to my father, have behaved as a friend to both him and Mama if she had not in truth been so? There would have been nothing to gain from such a deception. For the rest of the interlude I behaved as warmly and agreeably towards her as possible in an effort to make up for my unworthy thoughts of her.

It was after one of the reading lessons that I learned of the trouble between Jason and his father. I had seen the son a few times since that first meeting, not for very long ever, just long enough to exchange smiles and a few pleasantries. He was still a little shy, but always seemed pleased to see me. It came as a shock to hear that the quarrel still persisted. He did not, of course, attend the lessons as he had no need of them. His mother, educated by her clergyman father, had taught the boy herself.

On this particular evening Mrs. Colman approached me as I was packing away my books and slates and asked if I could spare a few more minutes as she wished to consult me about something. She took me into what was obviously the parlour and came straight to the heart of the matter. It was obvious from her expression that she was greatly troubled.

'You saw how it is,' she began at once. 'That first day in the kitchen, you saw how it is with Jason and his father...I read it in your face...' I could not deny the truth of what she was saying but I tried to minimise the situation.

'I saw your son looking angrily towards his father, if that is what you are referring to,' I agreed. 'But family disagreements are nothing out of the ordinary, I assure you. And love and affection usually re-assert themselves in every case. Such quarrels die as swiftly as they are born—'

'Not this one,' she interrupted. 'This goes deep.' There was a sadness and a deadly finality in her tone that served to alarm me. In some anxiety I remained silent and waited for her to continue.

'I'm at my wits end, Miss. I just don't know what to do about it. And I know I've no right to go troubling you with it, but I've nobody else to confide in...' She went on the explain that she was an only child and that her parents were long since

143

dead. She had no relatives in the county, just some distant cousins who lived in the north of Scotland.

'I've nobody close to me, nobody.' I told her that if she felt I could be of help, I would be happy for her to tell me about it.

'I know I can trust you, Miss,' she answered. 'I felt it straight away.' Wiping her eyes she told me the sad story.

'They never have got on well,' she began. 'Not since the lad grew up, that is. I don't rightly understand why, but they're different and yet too much alike, if you get my meaning.' I shook my head and replied that I didn't quite follow. She frowned.

'It's hard to explain,' she continued, 'but they're both that touchy, they flare up and say things I'm sure neither of 'em mean. They get angry, and that way they never come to understand each other.' I began to see what she meant.

'They are both very sensitive?' I suggested. 'Easily hurt or put out?'

'That's it,' she nodded. 'If only they would both keep calm when the arguments start—'

'But why do they argue at all, Mrs.

Colman? What causes the disagreements?'

'The music,' she replied to my astonishment.

'The music,' I echoed incredulously. 'What music?'

'Jason plays the violin,' she explained. 'He loves that fiddle more than anything in the world. His heart's in the music, not the farm...he, he wants to go away to learn properly—'

I remembered then that I had sometimes heard a violin being played somewhere in the house when I had come in the evenings. But I had paid little or no heed to it.

'And his father opposes the idea?'

'He won't hear of it, Miss. He's set on the lad carrying on the farm when he's gone. And he reckons it's only a craze that Jason's got: that he'll grow out of it.' I said I could see how difficult things must be for her. Loving them both, she must be torn between the two of them.

'But perhaps things will work out well in the end,' I suggested brightly, in an effort to cheer her. 'And I feel sure that you will be able to convince your son that his father has his interest at heart, and keep the peace between them.'

'That's what I've always told myself, Miss,' she replied. 'It's what kept me going. But you see I shalln't be here much longer.'

'Not here?' Whatever did she mean. She leaned back wearily on the horsehair sofa and it struck me suddenly that she must be near her time.

'The baby's due in a month,' she answered. 'And I'm going to die when it's born.'

For a moment I was speechless with shock. Then finding my voice I cried:

'Oh, no, Mrs. Colman. It cannot be so. You are mistaken to say such a thing—'

'There's no mistake,' she told me. 'I feel it here.' She laid a hand on her breast. 'And the doctor told me when Jason was born that there better hadn't be another. No, it'll be the end of me for sure.'

Assuming a briskness I was far from feeling, I tried to comfort her:

'It is your condition that causes you to be so despondent. At such times it is natural to become low in spirits. Believe me, when it is all over you will wonder how you could ever have entertained such thoughts.'

'Nay, lass,' she argued. 'What has to be

will be. And I do not fear death. It's what Jason'll do that torments me. He hates his dad now. What do you suppose he's going to be like when having this bairn kills me?'

'You mean,' I said slowly, 'that he will lay your death at his father's door?'

'I'm sure of it. Already he senses there's something not right with me. And oh, Miss, I'm sure I've seen murder in his eyes...' She broke off, sobbing uncontrollably.

Again I tried to comfort her: she was exaggerating the position I assured her. Jason would never do such a wicked, unspeakable deed. She must put the very idea out of her mind at once. Eventually she calmed down and seemed embarrassed that, as she put it, she had 'broken down'.

'But it's done me good to talk to you, Miss,' she sniffed. 'They do say that a trouble shared is a trouble halved, don't they?'

I left her with assurances that things were never quite as bad as they seemed and usually worked out for the best in the end.

'I have wondered about asking Mr. Southwold to have a word with Seth,' she announced suddenly as we walked to the garden gate. 'About the music I mean, but I didn't like in case the lad wasn't good enough—'

'I would very much like to hear your son play,' I interrupted her as an idea came to me. 'Do you think it could be arranged? I do have a certain knowledge of music—' Her face lit up.

'Then you could tell me if he *is* good enough,' she interrupted eagerly. 'Oh, Miss, that would be kind of you. I think the lad's good at it, but then I don't know much about these things really.' She went on to tell me that there was much about her son that puzzled her.

'He's a strange lad. He has a lot of talk about his music being an "extension of himself" and that he expresses his feelings through it.' She shook her head. 'I don't truly know what he means but I do try my best to understand him.'

'Do you think he will be agreeable to play for me?'

'I think so, Miss. Oh yes, I'm pretty sure of it. Especially if I explain what it might mean—'

'Don't build up his hopes too highly,' I warned. 'That would be cruel if he is not especially talented. On the other hand,' I added, seeing how her face fell, 'it may well be that your son has a rare gift and that there *is* a future for him in music.'

It was agreed that Jason be asked to play for me after the next reading lesson which was to take place in a few days time. It was gratifying to see how much happier Mrs. Colman looked at the decision. The look of desperation in her huge brown eyes had been replaced by one of hope and expectation. I too felt happier that evening than I had done for some time. As I rode home in the gig that was always despatched from Gales Hill to fetch me, a flicker of excitement stirred within me. If the boy was good, really good, and worthy of expert tuition, I could perhaps enlist the help of Edward Southwold in the matter. After all, Mr. Colman would be likely to take much more notice of his landlord than of me. It would be a chance to see him again. I almost wished I had arranged to hear Jason the very next day for the sooner I heard him, the sooner I might see Mr. Southwold...As it was I was impatient for the days to pass quickly till the appointed time.

But as things turned out I did not hear Jason play. Not then anyway. For before the day of my next visit to the farm arrived, Mrs. Colman was dead...

TEN

It was at her funeral that I saw Edward Southwold again. Across the small church our eyes met for a split second and my heart turned its customary somersault. In his black mourning clothes he looked, I thought, simply magnificent, more handsome and distinguished than ever. His expression as his gaze met mine, revealed nothing. Deep, intent yet unfathomable, it set my pulses racing. Confused and disconcerted I resolutely avoided looking in his direction for the rest of the service.

The church was full. The Colmans were a well-respected family, and farmers and their wives from a wide area of the Wolds were present. Lavinia and her mother were not there. They were in London. Lavinia had come to see me one morning very soon after my outing with Edward

Southwold to tell me about it. Her mother, it appeared, had suddenly decided that she, Lavinia, needed new gowns for the coming summer and that they must be purchased in London.

I had a faint suspicion that since my day with Mr. Southwold, Mrs. Lewis, who had learned of it no doubt with displeasure, looked on me as a rival to her daughter whom she was now determined should utterly outshine me in appearance.

'I am to have the very latest creations,' Lavinia announced excitedly, 'the most lavish and beautiful gowns that are to be had.'

'Where will you stay?' I had asked by way of showing interest.

'With relatives,' she'd answered promptly. 'I do not know them all that well as they are on Papa's side of the family. Mr. Graham-Lewis is a half-cousin or something of the kind of Papa's.'

Mr. Graham-Lewis! My heart sank. His wife had mentioned that he was a Yorkshireman I remembered, and had spoken of relatives in the county. I could not recall that she had ever told me their name, but even had she done so it would have meant nothing to me. For a moment

I wondered if I ought to tell Lavinia of my unfortunate experience with her distant relatives, but finally decided against doing so. It could well be that by now both Mr. and Mrs. Graham-Lewis had forgotten my very existence. They did not know where I lived, and it seemed most unlikely that my name would ever be mentioned. Better to let the past stay buried. I did think of asking Lavinia not to speak of me to them, but again changed my mind. It would only arouse her curiosity, and after all there was no reason to suppose that either she or her mother would make mention of me to their relatives. There would be no call to do so.

'Will it not be splendid?' Lavinia's voice had broken in on my thoughts. 'We are to stay for a few days and I can hardly wait for the time to come. I may be invited to parties and balls—oh it is all so exciting to contemplate.'

Had they been at home, it is unlikely that they would have attended Mrs. Colman's funeral. Mrs. Lewis, especially, considered the family beneath her notice. Although, allowing myself one final glance in the direction of Edward Southwold as he left the churchyard, it occurred to me suddenly that they might have attended, if only to come into contact with him for a short time.

Later that day, when I knew that the visiting mourners would have left, I walked down to the farm. I had been unable to erase from my mind the memory of Jason's face as he stood, pale of countenance but dry-eyed, beside his father. There had been a closed, withdrawn expression in his eyes that bothered me. He was too composed, too detached. He had, I knew, almost worshipped his mother and his total suppression of any outward sign of grief seemed unnatural to me. But when I reached the farm there was no sign of Jason. Mr. Colman said he had seen nothing of the boy since the funeral. Mrs. Fothergill, Polly's mother, who had made the tea for the mourners, agreed.

'He never came for a bite to eat,' she informed me. 'Not a bite. Where he's got to I don't know.' She shook her head ruefully. 'He's a strange one, that Jason, Miss, and no mistake, I can tell you.' I said I would call another time and left the house. Then as I walked past the great barn at the rear of the other farm buildings, I heard music coming from within. So that was where Jason was. I stopped, listening carefully, and held my breath in wonderment. For here, unless I was very much mistaken, was talent of the highest order. The boy was close to genius! The plaintive air continued, played with such feeling, such pathos as to move me to tears. Through his music Jason was expressing his grief, and I felt it as though it were my own. Had he always been able to play like this, I wondered, or had his present torment brought out, perhaps for the first time, the latent talent he had possessed all along? Could it be that the intense feelings he now experienced had given it life?

Suddenly the music stopped. I waited to see if it would begin again. But only silence came from the old barn. Then a different sound caught my ear; the sound of weeping. Jason had begun to sob as though his very heart was breaking, great racking sobs that seemed to tear him apart. I felt my own face wet with tears. The poor, lonely creature.

If only I could comfort him in some way. But I was uncertain how best to proceed. Should I leave him alone in his misery? Leave him to wrestle with his desolation of heart in privacy? Or should I go in to him? Let him see and know that someone cared that he suffered so? It was a difficult decision to have to make. In the end I decided that I must at least try to speak to him. Pushing open the great oak door I walked towards where Jason lay, face downwards, on a pile of old hay in the far corner. He obviously did not hear my footsteps and I was close beside him before he looked up and saw me. For a moment we stared at each other in silence. Somehow, what I felt towards him must have got through, for after a second a pathetic smile of welcome shone in his eyes. I prayed for the right words with which to ease his pain, the right words with which to bring comfort.

'Jason,' I began nervously. 'Believe me I know how you feel. My own mother died only a year ago, my father still more recently. I know it is hard to realise this just now, but the pain will ease, your heartache will grow less, in time.' There was no answer. I tried again.

'And you will see her again,' I told him. 'Death is not the end—'

'Of course it's the end.' This time, he

155

reacted violently to my words. 'I shall *never* see her again.'

'Jason,' I reasoned with him. 'You know you must not say such things. You know that the scriptures promise eternal life, do you not?'

'But I cannot believe it,' he cried unhappily. 'Oh, Helga, I *want* to believe it, but it seems so...so impossible. How can a dead person come alive again? Tell me that.'

Suddenly, blessedly, I firmly believe, I had an idea.

'Will you walk in the fields a little way with me Jason, please?' I asked him. 'There is something I wish to show you.' He looked surprised, but got at once to his feet.

'All right,' he agreed, and followed me out of the barn. Through the great stackyards we walked and out into the fields beyond. When we came to the first cornfield I stopped. Jason looked at me curiously. I put a hand on his arm.

'Look,' I began urgently. 'Do you remember when this field was sown with wheat?' He nodded uncomprehendingly. 'And do you remember how dead-looking the seed was?' Again Jason nodded, bewilderment still showing in his eyes.

'Yes, but—'

'Well look at it now Jason.' I cried, pointing over the field, a field that was a sheet of living green as the tender blades of corn reached and thrust upwards, straining towards the light and sun.

'Oh Jason, can't you see? Nothing really dies, it only changes, changes into something better. Death is but a gateway to another form of living.' The boy followed my gaze, and as I watched I saw some of the bewilderment leave his face.

'Picture the field as it will be at the harvest,' I urged him. 'Golden, abundant and beautiful. And so it will be with your mother, Jason. She has passed through death to life: to the light and warmth of a new existence, a higher consciousness whose dimensions we as yet cannot begin to imagine.'

Hope struggled on his face as he turned towards me.

'I think I understand what you wanted me to see,' he said quietly. 'And I try to believe it. But it doesn't bring her back. I want her *now*, not in some future life–*now*. I want to see her, talk to her...' he broke off and fell to his knees in the soft earth, sobbing. When he was calm again I said:

'Nothing can bring her back to us, not in that way. But part of her will be always with you: her love for you, her faith and belief in you. These things will live on in *you* if you'll only let them.' For a few seconds the boy was silent.

'She always understood,' he murmured at length. 'About the music, I mean...she saw what it meant to me—nobody else does—'

'Your father, you mean?' The conversation had taken the trend I had prayed for. It was essential, I felt, for Jason to bring into the open the black thoughts he harboured regarding this father.

'He *never* understood,' he went on bitterly. 'He cares about nothing but the farm. He has no interest in me, no real interest, he cares nothing how I think and feel. He sees me as somebody to work on the farm, nothing more. He doesn't love me and he didn't love my mother.'

'Jason!' I cried aghast at such a vicious tirade. 'You must not speak in this way. It is not true, not true at all. Your father is a good man. He loves you and he loved your mother dearly.' The boy stared at me, his eyes hard, his mouth twisted in bitterness.

Then a dull flush spreading over his face, he looked away from me, at the ground.

'He killed her, didn't he?' he asked with deadly quietness. I felt my own colour mounting. It was a delicate topic we now embarked upon. As Mrs. Colman feared, Jason blamed his father for her pregnancy and could not forgive him for it. My embarrassment was great and I did not know what to say. An awkward silence descended upon us. It was then that I saw the pistol. Lifted by a sudden gust of wind, Jason's cloak flew outwards and I saw the pistol jutting from one of his pockets. Greatly alarmed I had to decide without delay what to do about it. In his present mood the boy was clearly capable of murder. I stopped and looking him straight in the eye said urgently:

'That is not the answer, Jason.' He knew at once what I meant and did not pretend otherwise.

'He deserves to die,' he muttered harshly. 'He killed her. I hate him—'

'But your mother *loved* him,' I interrupted passionately. 'All she lived for was his good, his happiness, his and yours. If you kill your father and so destroy yourself, she will have lived in vain. And you wouldn't want that, would you, Jason, you loved her too much for that—'

'Well I'm glad the baby was dead,' he threw in savagely, but I could see that his dreadful resolve was weakening.

'Give it to me,' I suggested gently. 'Give the pistol to me, Jason, please.' I reached out to take it from his pocket but he caught my hand. I struggled with him, trying to get the deadly weapon away from him, when suddenly with a swift vehement gesture he pulled me close to him and kissed me savagely on the mouth. Shocked to the depths of my being I wrenched myself free of him, horrified at this totally unexpected turn of events.

'I love you.' Almost hysterical, Jason's eyes were wild. 'I love you, Helga. You talk to me as if I were a child and I can't stand it. I love you, I tell you, I love you.' And he tried to pull me to him once more. But I moved quickly away from him. A look of bitterness and anger crept into his eyes.

'It is as I thought,' he said with a kind of savage triumph. 'All these weeks, your smiles, your kind, sweet talk have meant nothing to you. It was all false. You do not love me, do you?' In spite of his hysteria, I knew I must be truthful.

160

'No Jason. I do not love you. I am fond of you and have a genuine desire to help you, that is all.'

'Then I shall kill myself,' he cried dramatically. 'Now that mother is gone there is nothing left to live for.'

'And your music?'

'It is nothing. I hate it.'

'Oh no you don't, Jason,' I argued passionately. 'You are upset now and do not know what you are saying. It is music you are in love with, not me. You have music in your soul. It is your very life. Some day you will be famous and all the world will clamour to hear you play.'

My words seemed to calm him a little and seizing my opportunity I suggested that we return to the barn and that he should play to me. Without a word he strode off in front of me. Once in the barn again, he picked up his violin. I cannot remember for how long he played. I only know that darkness was beginning to fall when he finally stopped. Without my asking, he took the pistol from his pocket and handed it to me. Then without a word he strode off towards the house.

Relieved that any immediate danger either to Jason or his father was over,

I followed him from the barn and made for the farm gate. In the gathering dusk, I saw a figure emerge from one of the sheds nearby. In my view only momentarily, it disappeared towards the house. It looked a little like Bessie and I supposed she was about her chores. Greatly troubled at Jason's outburst, I made my way homewards, agonising as to whether I was in any way to blame for it. I had never been any more than pleasant to the boy, I felt sure. He had read more into my smile, my words, that I had intended or could ever have imagined. So intent was I on my reflections that I didn't hear the carriage coming up the drive until it pulled up behind me at the foot of the steps. Lavinia and her mother, back from London, climbed down. They stared at me, disbelief on both their faces.

'What on earth are you doing with that pistol, Helga?' asked Mrs. Lewis severely. 'And where on earth have you been?' She was looking at me as if she couldn't believe her eyes. For the first time, I realised how dishevelled I must look. I glanced down at my muddy shoes, saw that my skirt was all crumpled and torn in one place, that there were wisps of hay clinging to its folds. Almost guiltily I hid the pistol behind my back.

'I...I found it,' I lied, unwilling to betray Jason. 'I found it in the lane.' And aware now that the coachman too was regarding me with round-eyed curiosity, I turned and ran up the steps and into my room.

Having tidied myself and changed my attire, I came downstairs again later on to find Lavinia and her mother in the drawing-room with Grandmother. Whether they had told her of our meeting at the entrance or not I did not know, but if she had learned of it, she gave no sign. The three of them were busy discussing the London visit. There was something different about Lavinia but I could not put a name to what the difference was. She seemed more alive somehow, more animated. Then shortly before they left, I found out. Grandmama declared she was tired and ready for bed, and at once Mrs. Lewis arose and escorted her to her room. The moment the door had closed behind them, Lavinia rushed across the room, flung her arms round my neck and declared that she had fallen in love.

'But...but Mr. Southwold...' I stammered. 'I thought—'

'Oh that.' Lavinia brushed her feeling for him aside as though it were non-existent. 'Hero worship, Helga. That's all *that* was. I know it now. Now that I'm truly in love.' As she spoke my heart leapt with joy and I listened bemused, dazed with happiness as she told me her story. She had, she confided, met this wonderful man, at the house of a friend. They had fallen in love with each other instantly. Her mother knew nothing of it and must not do so. Her mother would never approve. They planned to elope. Lavinia went on to say that she had given the man, Rupert was his name, my address and that letters from him to her, would come via myself. Opening her reticule she took out a piece of paper on which was a sample of his hand-writing. With this I could make no mistake about his letters. She would die, she declared, if I would not agree to act as their go-between. I looked down into the exquisite, pleading face. There was no doubting the intensity of her feelings. I had no hesitation in believing her love to be the real thing, and none either in agreeing to her plan. Lavinia then went on to explain that she might for a time have to pretend in front of her mother that she was still attracted to Mr. Southwold, so as not to arouse her suspicions.

'And such a deception can do no harm,' she finished. 'For in truth, I know that he has no love for me. He is fond of me in the same way a father is fond of a daughter. He will know how to handle it.' I smiled. She was right of course. It would be difficult, I mused inwardly, to imagine any situation which Edward Southwold could not handle.

My hope that night was strong. Now at last I was free to reveal my love. Oh, not by word of course, unless joy of joys, he should declare himself, but by gesture, glance, attitude. And tomorrow I would see him. For I had resolved earlier, after the incident with Jason, to solicit Edward's help on behalf of the boy. Tormented, mixed up and troubled as Jason was, he needed help quickly. I could vouch personally for the boy's musical talent now, and I had decided to try to persuade Edward to use his influence with Mr. Colman with a view to Jason being properly taught. And I felt confident that he would hear me sympathetically. Whether or not to tell him of Jason's passionate declaration of love for me, I could not quite make up my mind. I knew I could trust Edward, that he would treat the matter as being in the strictest confidence, but I was not sure that I had the right to confide Jason's secret, even to him. Then, pushing the pistol further out of sight beneath my clothes in the drawer where I had earlier hastily concealed it, I decided that I ought to tell him. The sooner Jason went away the better. And if Edward knew the whole of the boy's problems, he would be all the more inclined to act on his behalf. In any case, it would be wrong I felt, to enlist his help, without telling him the whole story.

On rising the next morning I went at once to Grandmother's room and told her of my plans. Of Jason's feelings towards me I said nothing. I concentrated on his talent, stressing the fact that he needed the best possible tuition, and my belief that Edward Southwold could persuade Mr. Colman to agree. She did not appear to be very interested, but she said I did right to consult Mr. Southwold if the matter worried me. But she couldn't imagine what the world was coming to, she went on. Farmer's sons wanting to be musicians indeed! What next pray? Why couldn't people accept their proper station in life any more? That was what she would like to know, and so on and so forth. No good could come of such new-fangled ideas as were being expressed these days. And she hoped that I had not been filling the young man's head with a lot of foolish notions that might only lead to disappointment in the end. I repeated that I firmly believed that Jason possessed tremendous talent, and as soon as possible, took my leave of her. In the doorway I almost collided with Francis. Reaching out to steady me, he put an arm round my waist, holding me rather longer and more closely than was necessary. As I pulled away from him he favoured me with an odd sort of look, bold and slightly suggestive. It annoyed me a trifle, but I thought that he perhaps still suffered the effects of being in his cups the night before. Anxious to start for the Hall, I did not linger and paid little heed to the matter. Downstairs, I ordered the gig to be brought round to the front entrance and then realised that I had left my reticule in my bedchamber. I ran upstairs again and as I passed by Grandmother's room I could hear Francis talking with her. It was hearing my own name mentioned that caused me to stop. Perhaps I should not have done so, but it was an involuntary reaction.

'I hear that Helga came in with her skirt torn last night,' Francis was saying. I did not wait to hear more, but cheeks aflame, sped silently past. Something in his tone had left me in little doubt as to what he was surmising! No wonder he had given me that strange look. Perhaps I ought to have been completely frank about the whole matter so that misconceptions of this kind could not have arisen. But I still felt that I could not betray Jason. I would just have to suffer any innuendoes Francis might make, or questions from Grandmother, as best I could. I was innocent of any reprehensible behaviour I reminded myself, and that truth always wins in the end.

At the front door I found the idiot boy hanging about the gig. He wanted to come with me, it was plain by the look on his face. The boy tended to follow me about a lot, almost like a dog, and to be taken along for a ride in any of the carriages with me seemed to delight him enormously. The groom, a good-natured lad, smiled tolerably as on my indicating that he might do so, the idiot boy climbed up beside him.

It was my first visit to the Hall and my heart beat nervously as we approached the lodge gates. My mind flew back to the night of my arrival in Yorkshire. I wondered if the old lodge-keeper and his wife would stare at me as they had done on that occasion. What they had said that night had gone completely from my thoughts, but now it returned to me in full force. They had said I would bring trouble. Well I had not done so. They could see that for themselves. This time no doubt they would behave differently: they would nod and smile in welcome. But I was mistaken. There was no smile, no welcome on the face of the old man as he swung the gates apart, nor on that of his wife as she watched from the lodge door. My own smile of greeting froze on my face. Then I lifted my head in a haughty fashion. Let them stare their fill, I told myself. I would refuse to be upset or made to feel uneasy by such people. The idiot boy sensed something. I could tell by the way his gaze darted from them to me and back again. His poor befuddled brain was trying to understand the situation. He felt, I believe, that I was upset over something and it bothered him.

The groom, a placid, stolid and unimaginative youth, concerned only with the horse, was oblivious to any atmosphere. The gig continued up the long avenue, an avenue bordered by tall limes, and as we grew nearer to the great gothic mansion towering before us, all thoughts of the incident left my mind. I was so nervous when the gig finally pulled up at the foot of the wide sweeping terrace that I trembled in every limb. It was a mild morning yet I shivered: shivered with hope, suspense, dread almost.

What if Edward Southwold refused to receive me? Or what if, having agreed to see me, he were to treat me coldly as though I were nothing more to him than a casual acquaintance? I pulled myself together, told the groom to wait, got down from the gig and climbed the steps to the front door.

A man-servant, somewhere in the middle years, answered my summons. I wondered if he too, would stare at me, but to my relief my appearance seemed to mean nothing to him. From his speech I knew he was not a native of the county for he sounded like people I had talked to in the south. I was politely requested to step into the entrance hall and to wait while he found out if 'the master' would see me. Within less than a minute he returned with the news that Mr. Southwold would see me immediately in the morning-room. My heart thudded so wildly in my breast as I followed him that I thought he must surely hear it, and when he threw open the door and announced me I was worked up to such a state of suspense that I burned as though from some fever. Summoning up all of my self-control I walked into the room.

Edward Southwold was seated behind a large oak desk. He rose at once and came to meet me, a smile of welcome on his face. I smiled up at him shyly in return and as I took his proffered hand a thrill of sheer delight coursed through me. When we were both seated he asked what he could do for me.

'I have come to ask your help in a matter of some urgency,' I told him and went on to recount the whole story. He heard me out without comment and then to my immense joy, said that of course he would help the boy. He would ride over to see Colman and Jason that very day and see what could be arranged.

'If the boy is as talented as you believe, he must go to Europe to study, and in any case, I agree with you that for him to remain where he is would be extremely inadvisable under the circumstances.' I stood up.

'I don't know how to thank you, Sir,' I began. 'I have been so troubled over the matter, so anxious for dear little Mrs. Colman's sake, to help—'

'You can thank me, Miss Radford,' he cut me short, 'by sitting down again and agreeing to remain a little longer. There is one point which I wish to discuss with you in more detail.'

My heart leapt for joy. There was nothing in the world I wished for more than to remain in his presence.

'With great pleasure, Mr. Southwold,' I agreed warmly.

'There is one matter I want to be absolutely certain about,' he began. 'you dismiss Jason's feelings for you as infatuation. How can you know that?'

'I have seen infatuation before, Mr.

172

Southwold,' I replied without hesitation. 'The boy is in love with love, he will quickly outgrow it. In fact I doubt whether in normal circumstances he would ever have made such an outburst. He was over-wrought, strung to breaking point and hardly aware of what he was saying.'

'And *your* feelings for him? You are deeply concerned for him I can see. Concern and love often go hand in hand.' He was watching me carefully as he spoke, his eyes raking my face.

'I am not in love with Jason,' I told him steadily. 'Such an idea is laughable.'

'He is a handsome young man of your own age, Miss Radford. The idea is far from laughable, I assure you.'

'I am absolutely certain that I do not love him,' I repeated.

'How can you be so sure?'

'Because,' I began confidently, unaware of the trap I was falling into, 'it is impossible to mistake true love—' I stopped abruptly. Too late, I realised what I had implied. Blushing furiously I looked away from him, unable to meet that searching gaze one moment longer.

'So,' he murmured softly, remorselessly,

'you have *known* true love, Miss Radford?' My eyes fixed firmly on the floor I did not answer him. 'Come now, little Helga,' he insisted still more softly, moving round the desk and standing closer to me, 'I asked you a question. It is impolite not to answer.' Suddenly I knew that he was teasing me, lovingly, teasing me into an admission of my feelings for him. And such behaviour could mean but one thing: he loved me! My heart almost burst with joy.

Throwing caution to the winds I looked full into his face.

'Yes,' I cried happily, and in the full knowledge that my eyes must be shining for sheer love of him. 'Yes, Mr. Southwold, I have known, still do know, real, true love.' Still continuing to tease me, he took my hands and drew me to my feet.

'And the object of this love, the man concerned, he is in Germany perhaps?' I sensed the loving laughter behind the dark, unsmiling eyes.

'He is in England,' I replied equally seriously, keeping up the game.

'Not in Yorkshire?'

'In Yorkshire.'

'And do I know this luckiest of all men, my dear little Helga?' His arms were now about my waist. His dark head bent close to mine.

'Better than anyone in the world, I should imagine,' I reponded softly. With a cry of triumph he pulled me tightly to him and, as our lips met I felt the hard fast beating of his heart against my breast. For a moment time stood still, as aflame with passion, our bodies strained together.

'We shall marry as soon as it can be arranged,' he told me thickly, as we drew apart. 'I will have the engagement announced today.'

It was time to leave. Hand in hand we walked to the entrance. Outside, a strange sight greeted us. The idiot boy was walking up and down beside the gig, his body affecting a grotesque stoop, his usually blank but jovial expression replaced by an ugly grimace. The groom was laughing heartily at his antics which seemed to please the lad enormously.

'What on earth—?' began Edward.

'It's all right,' I interrupted, smiling, as it dawned on me what the charade was about.

'Jimmy is a born mimic. He just cannot help it. And I'm afraid that at this moment he is imitating your lodge-keeper. He did stare at me rather alarmingly as we came through the gates. His wife did too,' I added. Something in my tone must have revealed to him that the incident had upset me.

'There is no need to let their stares worry you, my darling,' he whispered softly.

'But why do they do so?' It really did trouble me.

'Why, because you are so beautiful,' he replied lightly. 'How can they help but stare?'

It was a pleasing and flattering explanation and I dearly wanted to accept it as the truth. I smiled up at him warmly and let the matter drop, determined to forget it. But I could not do so. In spite of my new-found joy and ecstasy, my thoughts kept harking back to those staring faces. It was not my so-called beauty that caused the old couple to look at me as they did. It was something else, I sensed. Something that boded no good for me. I felt suddenly cold as though some dark cloud shadowed my path...

ELEVEN

But events moved with such speed from that day onwards that I had little time to dwell upon the matter.

Mrs. Lewis took the news of my betrothal much better than I had anticipated. She admitted that she had at one time nursed hopes of Lavinia becoming Mrs. Edward Southwold, but it was of no consequence. During the London visit she had realised that her daughter would never be short of suitors and that she could count at least two titled gentlemen amongst her many admirers, already. Behind her mother's back, Lavinia flashed me a knowing smile. Later she confided that she was relieved at not having to keep up the pretence of favouring Mr. Southwold any more.

'I doubt if I could have done it, Helga,' she sent on. 'It would have been uncommonly difficult, with my heart, my thoughts and my dreams somewhere else.'

It would indeed, I agreed. Mrs. Lewis said that I must leave all the arrangements for the wedding in her hands: even though she was not a relative, she felt like one, having been brought up with my father.

'I shall, naturally, consult your grandmother about everything,' she added. It sounded almost like an afterthought and I wondered suddenly if Grandmama ever resented Mrs. Lewis's managing ways. She was not, in spite of her age and her disability, the sort of person to take kindly to being 'managed'. But strangely enough, Grandmama seemed relieved to delegate all responsibility for the affair to Mrs. Lewis. She was, she declared, too old to want to bother her head with it. It was an attitude one could understand and yet, knowing her as I did, I felt there was something more behind it, for I sensed a sudden coldness on her part towards me, a coldness which both hurt and puzzled me. I wondered what I could have done to displease her and could think of nothing, unless—but no, it was too ridiculous even to contemplate...or was it? Francis had told her of my torn skirt. Perhaps she had read into the incident as much as he had obviously done. Grandmama was extremely strait-laced. The least suspicion of improper behaviour would be anathema to her. It was a trifle worrying but I consoled myself with the thought that I was perhaps exaggerating or imagining things. And surely if she did harbour reservations as to my propriety, straightforward person as she was, she would have lectured me on the subject.

There were no further innuendoes from Francis, I was relieved to find. He seemed genuinely pleased at my betrothal to Edward and declared that when he was a beggar, as he felt he undoubtedly would end up some day, he would present himself at my lordly gates to beg for bread. Poor Francis, he was really such an ass in some ways, but he could always be relied upon to make me laugh and I felt that he liked me in his own uncaring, shallow way. He still spent most of his time away somewhere, but during the times he was at home I began to notice that he seemed often to be talking to Polly. It was nothing to do with me of course but I hoped that he was not encouraging the poor girl too much. Polly liked him, I knew and I just hoped that she wasn't getting too deeply involved with him. One morning I came across them talking earnestly together on a corner of the landing but they hurriedly went about their separate ways at my approach.

Actually I was in fact so happy during those first days after my betrothal that I did not worry or think about anything for very long. All I thought of was Edward, my dearest, darling husband-to-be. I was almost delirious with happiness, so much so that sometimes I knew a sudden, swift fear that it was too great to last, that I was living in a fool's paradise...

True to his word Edward had seen Mr. Colman and Jason the very day I had visited the Hall and had talked Mr. Colman into allowing his son to go abroad to study music. To my great joy, Germany had been the country Edward had decided upon and he had made arrangements for Jason to be a pupil under one of the country's leading musicians. He had also decided to take the boy himself.

'I intended to journey to the Continent later this month on business,' he had told me. 'I will simply bring the visit forward.'

It was wonderful news as far as Jason was concerned and indeed was in a sense what I had hoped for, but at the thought of Edward's going away my heart sank. The night before he left I clung to him passionately.

'Take me with you,' I begged.

Putting me gently from him, 'And ruin your reputation?' he teased. 'No, my love, it cannot be. Your grandmother would never permit such indiscretion.'

'I shall count the days,' I whispered, 'the hours too.'

'And I also,' he returned ardently.

I had seen nothing of Jason since the night of his mother's funeral. I had been to the farm once or twice since then to give the farmhands their lessons but not once had I encountered him. Whether it was by pure chance or whether he felt embarrassed and did not wish to see me, I did not know. But on the day of departure I decided to seek him out. With all my heart I wished him well and I wanted him to know that. For his dear little mother's sake too, I felt I could not let him leave without saying farewell. Edward had told me the hour at which he would call at the farm for the boy and so I presented myself there some few minutes before the Hall carriage was due to appear.

I found Jason tense, nervous, a little strained but obviously excited. Neither he nor I made any reference to his behaviour on our last meeting and after an initial embarrassment he soon relaxed. There was still an air of constraint between him and his father, I noted, but at least they seemed on better terms than they had been. It was expedient though that they were to be parted, I felt. The farmhands were all assembled to see Jason off, as were Mrs. Fothergill and Bessie, Polly's sister. The two women were both in tears and Mrs. Fothergill was full of motherly admonitions to the boy and warnings to 'watch out for himself' among 'them foreigners'. She behaved almost as if he were going to live among some heathen nation of savages. Bessie said nothing, but tears trickled silently down her white face as she stood there looking at Jason. Then as the carriage trundled out of the yard and we all waved our farewells I suddenly felt her gaze upon me. Her eyes were hard and bitter. When she realised that I was aware of her scowling she turned and walked hurriedly into the house.

I felt disturbed. I had given Jason a sisterly kiss on the cheek on parting but surely that could not have upset the girl. Surely she did not imagine there was anything between Jason and myself. In any case she knew of my betrothal to

Edward. Why had she looked at me with such hatred? I had gathered from remarks made both by her mother and by Polly that Bessie was, as they put it, 'sweet on' Jason, but it was ludicrous to imaging that she saw me as a rival. Then realisation dawned on me. It was because Jason was going to Germany. She blamed me for taking him away from her. I felt sorry for the girl, truly sorry, and yet I felt that if she really cared for the boy, she would not wish to stand in his light.

I had meant that day to return Jason's pistol to him. It had occurred to me that he might like to have it with him on his travels. But I had forgotten it. In a quiet moment when I had been able to speak to him alone I had mentioned the matter and suggested that I return to Gales Hill to get it for him. He had told me there was no need.

'I have another one. Keep it until I return.'

But later, when I opened my drawer to put away my gloves, I saw that the pistol had gone. I stared in consternation and disbelief. Where could it have got to? I sat down on the bed to think things over. A firearm was not an object one easily mislaid. Someone had removed it from my drawer. The question was whom? And for what purpose? The connotations of such a question were not pleasant. In my mind I went through the people, besides Jason, who knew that I had it: Lavinia and her mother, the coachman, Edward and Grandmama. But of them only my grandmother lived in the house. Lavinia and her mother had the run of it, true, but they would not enter my room. They were the sort of people too, I reckoned, who would probably be terrified of touching such a lethal object. That Grandmama should have taken it was out of the question.

Suddenly I remembered about the mystery of the pressed flowers in my journal. Could the person concerned in that incident be the one who had removed the pistol? I had half-suspected Polly of the former but as there had been no repitition of it, I had not questioned her. This, however, was a much more serious affair. I pulled the bell-rope and waited for her to answer my summons. I did not relish my task. I had noticed of late a certain coldness towards me on Polly's part which both puzzled me and bothered me a little, and to have to question her in this manner was not likely to improve our relationship.

'Polly,' I began gently, as soon as she appeared, anxious to upset her as little as possible, 'have you, in the course of cleaning my room at any time, seen a pistol?'

'No, Miss,' she replied coldly.

'It was in here,' I walked over to the the dressing-table and indicated the top drawer. At my words a dull flush stained the girl's cheeks. She drew herself up haughtily and answered indignantly that she wasn't in the habit of prying into people's drawers.

'Believe me, Polly,' I assured her, distressed at her reaction, 'I am not accusing you of any such act. I just thought that you might have put a scarf or something away for me at some time, seen the pistol, and thought it ought to be put in the gunroom, or something.' She looked at me sulkily.

'Well I haven't,' she repeated, 'and I don't like being accused of taking things out of drawers. I've never touched nothing what didn't belong to me in all my life.'

'Of course you haven't, Polly dear.' I

tried to mollify her. 'And I'm deeply sorry if I have offended you.' The girl sniffed.

'If that's all, Miss Radford,' she said stonily, 'I'll get back to the kitchen.' Head high, cheeks red, she stalked out of the room. I felt upset, and wished I had left the matter alone. The only thing I had achieved through my questioning was to make an enemy of the girl. I was convinced that she had spoken the truth. It was not Polly who had taken the pistol, or read my journal. Someone else had secretly entered my bedchamber and opened my drawer.

Who could it be, and what did it all mean? The staring faces of the old lodge couple flashed before my eyes and I felt once more the chill of fear upon my heart. The cloud was darker now, and drawing closer...

That night sleep eluded me. The atmosphere was close, like thunder I thought, and I got out of bed and sat for a while beside the open window. I did not light my candle but sat there in the darkness trying to dispel the unease that troubled my spirit. I longed for Edward, for the feel of his arms around me, for the comfort and strength, the feeling of security that his very presence afforded me.

All at once I became aware of voices in the garden below. Francis and Mrs. Lewis were talking together.

'It will work.' Francis was speaking. 'My gambling will seem as nothing to this in her eyes.'

'Well do not involve me,' replied his companion. 'And remember it may be...' They moved out of earshot and the rest was lost to me. What I had heard meant nothing to me. Idly I wondered if it concerned some lady-friend or other that Francis had, then dismissed the matter from my thoughts. But hearing his voice like that suddenly brought back to my mind the memory of another occasion on which I had overheard it: the morning he had mentioned my torn skirt to Grandmama. I had forgotten all about that. Now, remembering, I realised the significance of it. He had not seen me for himself. Someone else had told him about my dishevelled appearance. And it followed, surely, that whoever had informed him of the matter would also have mentioned the pistol...Perhaps it was Francis who had secretly entered my room and taken the weapon from my drawer...But why, for heaven's sake? He had pistols of his own. What could he want with this one? And if he did need it for some reason, why not ask me openly for it? Oh it was all so worrying and confusing, I just did not know what to make of the situation and what to do about it. I could hardly go to him and accuse him of going through my drawers. I could search the house, I supposed, but I felt that such a course of action would be futile. If the pistol had been taken secretly, it was hardly likely that it would have been left about openly...

The next day a letter arrived from London. Addressed to me, I knew at once from the handwriting that it was really for Lavinia. After breakfast I took it over to her and luckily found her alone.

'Mama is busy writing in the morning-room,' she whispered, her eyes dancing with joy as she took the letter from my hand. 'Oh, Helga, I would have died if he had not written soon,' she declared. Understanding how desperately eager to read the letter she was, I told her that I wanted to return home immediately and she did not try to persuade me to do otherwise. At the entrance she gave me a quick hug and declared that I was the best friend anybody could ever have. Later that day I saw her again and after confiding the contents of the letter had lived up to her fondest expectations, she went on to ask me if I had noticed any change in her mother at all.

'Your mother?' I was surprised.

'Yes,' she replied. 'There is something different about her. She is excited. I know it. But what about I cannot imagine. Her life is so dull, so predictable.' I remembered the conversation I had overheard in the garden. Come to think of it, Mrs. Lewis *had* sounded a little excited. But I said nothing of this to Lavinia.

'It is almost,' Lavinia was saying, 'almost as if she were in love—'

'Would that be so strange? Your mother is not so old.'

'For her it would be most strange,' came the reply. 'Please do not misunderstand me when I say this, Helga, for I am very fond of dear Mama, but she is cold—'

'She must have loved your father?' Lavinia shook her head.

'Perhaps I should not tell you, Helga, but you are like a sister to me and I cannot keep things from you, but from what I heard once, Mama only married Papa for his wealth. He was many years her senior.'

'She could still have loved him,' I protested.

'No.' Lavinia seemed sure. 'I do not think so.' She came closer to me and lowered her voice to a whisper.

'You know the old lodge-keeper at the Hall? Well, his wife visits cook sometimes and once I heard her saying that the only thing Mama loved about my father was his money.'

'Servants' gossip,' I told her severely. 'Really, Lavinia, I am amazed that you should give any credence whatever to such idle talk.' The poor girl looked sheepish at my admonition.

'Perhaps you are right,' she admitted. 'But sometimes I cannot help but wonder about her. More so especially now that I am in love myself.' I looked at her questioningly, at a loss to follow her line of thought.

'It is just that things keep coming back to me,' she explained. 'Things from my childhood. Like coming across Mama secretly weeping–'

'But naturally so,' I interrupted. 'After your father died.'

'It was *before* he died,' she said slowly.

'And that wasn't all, Helga. After Papa died she sometimes left the house late at night...and I have seen her do it again, recently...'

'Are you sure?'

Lavinia nodded.

'Yes. And she has started the talking again—'

'Started the talking? What on earth do you mean?'

'She used to do it sometimes when I was little,' Lavinia explained. 'I would hear her talking as if someone were with her in her room, *but there was nobody there*. Last night I heard her again...'

'Lots of lonely people talk to themselves,' I replied lightly. 'I am sure that it all it amounts to.'

But after we had parted I found myself wondering about what Lavinia had confessed to me. In spite of her kindness towards me I had never truly liked Mrs. Lewis. Something about her, just what, I could not exactly determine, had repelled me slightly. But now, in the light of this new knowledge of her past, I felt a certain compassion towards her. Perhaps her loneliness had soured and hardened her. Perhaps she had been disappointed with her lot. There is a sense, I supposed, in which we are what life has made of us. And yet, I reasoned, is it not true that it is what we ourselves make of the circumstances of our lives that really determines the sort of people we become? Two people subjected to identical hardship or sorrow might react in totally different ways...

All the same, whatever her trouble had been and whatever her response, I now felt that I understood her a little better. And I reflected (and felt guilty about it) how easy it is, through ignorance, to misjudge one's fellows.

A few days later such reflections took on for me a new and terrible significance. For this time it was I who was being misjudged...misjudged without mercy and pronounced guilty...

TWELVE

To the day I die I shall never forget that night. I even remember the exact time, for the chiming-clock on the landing struck the hour of nine as I walked to the drawing-room in response to Grandmother's summons.

The scene that met my eyes as I entered the room is indelibly stamped upon my memory. To this very day I can see in my mind's eye Grandmama sitting in her blue brocade chair, her back stiff and proud, her mouth set in a hard, angry line. By her side stood Francis, his expression unusually serious. In his hand he held a letter. On the couch a few yards away sat Mrs. Lewis, her face flushed. She did not meet my gaze. The smile of greeting froze on my face. Something told me that this was no time for smiling. Apprehension stirred in my heart. This was no ordinary summons. Nervously I cleared my throat.

'You wish to speak to me, Grandmama?' My voice sounded strained and unnatural even to my own ears.

'I most certainly do,' she answered haughtily. 'You wicked, wicked girl—'

'Now, Aunt Louise,' Mrs. Lewis had risen at the outburst and gone and laid a restraining hand on grandmother's arm, 'you must not work yourself up into such a state. It is not good for you. And as I've already told you, it may be lies.'

'What may be lies?' Shaken to the core,

I at last found my voice. 'What is all this?' I looked wildly round at them all, 'What is the matter?'

'You may well ask, madam, you may well ask,' Grandmother flung at me. Then turning towards Francis: 'Show her, Francis, show her what is the matter.' In silence Francis handed me the letter. Trembling with fear I started to read it. It was addressed to Grandmother and bore no signature. With mounting anger and dismay I read the poisonous, sick-making accusations. The writer alleged that I was guilty of 'loose and improper conduct of a scandalous nature', with Jason Colman and with at least one of the farm-hands. I had been seen, the letter went on, in the most compromising circumstances. I felt my face go white with shock and disgust. I was so angry that for a moment I could not speak.

'Well, what have you to say?' Grandmama hissed at me. I threw the letter on to the floor. Somehow I managed to control my temper.

'It is a lie,' I replied coldly. 'An iniquitous lie from beginning to end. And that you could even begin to believe such things both astounds and wounds me to

194

the depths of my being.'

For a moment or two Grandmama remained silent, as though she were considering my denial. I appealed to the other two.

'Surely you believe me?' I asked. 'You must know that it is untrue–'

'Of course.' Mrs. Lewis came to my rescue. 'Of course it is untrue, Helga dear. I have told them so all along—'

'And you, Francis, you believe me don't you?' He was silent for a moment and than a bold, almost insulting look on his face, shook his head.

' 'Fraid not, old girl,' he replied half-apologetically. 'You see I had wind of...of your...your goings on some time ago from Polly—'

'From Polly?' I was absolutely thunderstruck. 'From Polly? What on earth are you talking about–'

'And then, there's always the other little matter—' Francis went on as though I hadn't spoken.

'Now, Francis, shut up,' interrupted Mrs. Lewis. 'I forbade you to mention it, ever—'

'Mention what?' Grandmama demanded. 'What have you been hiding from me

Emma? Tell me at once.'

'What she has been hiding from you,' Francis began, 'is that your granddaughter, our 'little innocent' Helga here was dismissed from the Graham-Lewis household, for improper conduct. That because of that dismissal she could find no other post in London. That was why she came here.' White with rage Grandmother rose to her feet.

'I might have known,' she shouted at me. 'I might have known what to expect from the daughter of a common governess. And to think that I believed in you, that I altered my will in your favour. You slut, you hussy. It is only because it is night that I do not order you from my house this very moment. You will leave at first light in the morning.'

'Oh, Aunt Louise, don't be so harsh, I beg you,' Mrs. Lewis was beside her again. 'Give poor Helga a chance to explain, she may be innocent, in fact I feel sure she is—'

'You're a fool, Emma.' Grandmother silenced her. 'You always were. Trusting to the last. Begging for Helga just as you did for her scheming baggage of a mother—'

'Stop,' I shouted, my temper out of control at this slur on my mother. 'How dare you speak so of Mama? I could kill you for it. She was worth ten thousand of such as you...you stiff-necked arrogant snob. Say or think what you will of me, I no longer care, but I will not have my mother slandered.'

Grandmother ignored my outburst. She addressed Francis.

'Send for Adams first thing tomorrow. The will must be changed back again without delay. I would rather my money go to a gambler than a harlot.' She almost choked over the final word, breathing heavily, and I thought she was going to suffer a heart attack. But her indisposition was momentary and she quickly returned to the attack.

'I shall deem it my duty to inform Mr. Southwold,' she told me icily. 'It is only right that he should know of your conduct. What he does about it, is his affair. As for me, I shall *never* forgive you. You have dragged the name of Radford, one of the oldest, most honoured names in England, into the gutter. I shall go to my grave hanging my head in shame.'

I knew it was useless to deny this second

accusation. Why, if I were innocent, had I not told her of the incident when I first arrived, Grandmama would demand. Why keep such a thing hidden unless I were to blame? In a sense I think she *wanted* to find me guilty. It gave her some justification I expect for the way she had treated Mama. I knew that nothing that I could say would make the slightest difference. Without another word I walked from the room. As I opened the door I almost bumped into Polly. She scuttled off in haste on seeing me. I remember thinking that she must have been listening at the keyhole. With a part of me I supposed I ought to round on her, demand what she meant by her false tales, but a terrible ennervating weariness had descended upon me, and I let her go.

Francis came to my chamber as I was packing my trunk. He suddenly appeared in the open doorway, watching me. I ignored him. I felt I did not know him any more, he was like a stranger. After a minute or so he spoke.

'I'm sorry the old girl took it to heart so,' he began. 'I didn't think she would turn you out.'

'You are not a bit sorry,' I replied. 'You

made it worse, you with your lies about my "goings-on".' He stared at me with a hateful, knowing smirk.

'Come off it, old girl. There's no need to keep up the pretence with me. I know all about that time in the barn with Jason...the night you came in covered with hay...soon tired of him though, didn't you, when a bigger fish showed interest—'

'Get out,' I ordered furiously. 'Get out and don't ever speak to me again.'

'Now don't take it like that,' the tone he used was sick-making. 'I know what you continentals are. I've known one or two in my time, down in London. Don't think I blame you. Have a bit of fun while you can, that's my motto. I wouldn't have given you away normally. But when I found out that she'd altered the will in your favour, well, something had to be done about it...That money should be mine. Why else do you suppose I have stayed in this God-forsaken hole all these years? I want it. *All of it.*' And with that he left me.

I had not been alone more than a couple of minutes before there was a knock on my door. It was Mrs. Lewis. She seemed very upset, declaring she would never forgive herself for having 'let slip' to Francis about Mr. Graham-Lewis and myself.

'It doesn't matter,' I replied listlessly. 'Francis has admitted that he intended to set Grandmother against me, come what may. Knowledge of the London incident and the arrival of the letter just helped his plans, that's all.' I was reaching for my cloak as I spoke. Mrs. Lewis put out a restraining hand.

'You are not leaving now, Helga?' I nodded.

'I do not wish to remain in this house a moment longer.'

'Oh, Helga, I beg you do not behave so hastily. By tomorrow morning your grandmother may have had second thoughts. I do not believe she can be so cruel as to turn you on to the streets. Pray wait a little.' I shook my head.

'Come to the Dower House,' she pleaded. 'At least for a while, until you are able to make further plans.'

'It is uncommonly good of you to suggest it,' I told her, 'but it would not do. I have no wish to promote ill-feeling between Grandmother and yourself.'

'Just for tonight, then,' she urged. 'You cannot leave at this time of night.'

I was suddenly aware of how desperately tired I was.

'Very well,' I agreed, taking off my cloak. 'I will stay until it is daylight, but here, in my own chamber. Please say goodbye to Lavinia for me.'

Seemingly satisfied, Mrs. Lewis took her leave of me. She did not offer to kiss me. She held out her hand and as I took it she looked at me in a strange and penetrating manner. Then shaking her head she turned and left me, muttering something to herself. It sounded like: *I cannot see anything of you, my dear.* As it made no sense to me whatever I assumed I had misheard what she said.

I undressed and got into bed but was unable to sleep. The events of the evening kept going round and round in my tortured brain. My wretchedness and misery were too deep for tears and I lay dry-eyed staring into the darkness above me. What had I done, I asked myself, what heinous sin had I committed that life should have treated me so unjustly? Not that I cared one fig about losing Grandmama's fortune: it meant nothing to me and I had been ignorant of the fact that I was to inherit it. No, what tore at my heart was what

Edward would think of me. I would not be here when he returned, and Grandmama would waste no time in contacting him and telling him all that had been recounted to her. I could see that, innocent though I was, I had perhaps behaved foolishly through my ignorance of English ways. It had never once occurred to me that my actions might be misconstrued. I myself had seen no harm in keeping the brightest of the farm lads a little longer than the others, or in being in the barn that night with Jason...Others, Bessie no doubt, and perhaps her mother and sister had seen such ways in a very different light, as had Francis and in turn Grandmother. Would they, I wondered bitterly, have been so swift to believe such things had I been completely English? Or did the fact that I had a 'foreign' mother half condemn me to begin with?

Supposing Edward doubted me... My heart went cold as the terrible possibility of it broke me down. I wept at last, wept because my heart was breaking and all of life seemed too heavy for me to bear. The tears brought relief and finally I slept.

I awoke suddenly, as if some noise had startled me. But all was silent. The sleep had refreshed and strengthened me and I felt more capable of facing whatever lay ahead of me. I lay back among the pillows thinking things over. Suddenly I sat bolt upright as something hit me for the first time. The writing in that anonymous letter! I had seen it somewhere before, I was sure of it. But where? I racked my brains but to no avail. Try as I might I could not remember. But there was something I *did* remember. It suddenly came into my mind. The conversation between Francis and Mrs. Lewis. I could recall some of the very words.

'Don't involve me,' Mrs. Lewis had said, so, *she had known what Francis was up to.* Had known all along and had not given me one word of warning. I felt sick to my stomach at the way she had deceived me. And I could not understand it. It seemed obvious to me now that she hated me because of my betrothal to Edward and was just an anxious as Francis was, to discredit me, albeit for a different reason. But why the pretence? What did she hope to gain from her false behaviour? Declaring her belief in me! Begging me for my own good to stay the night, indeed! Was she, I wondered, one of those people who seek to do evil to their victims and cunningly see to it that the blame is laid at the door of another? If so she was beneath contempt. Disgusted and sick at heart, I flung off the bedcovers and got up. I would leave this accursed place now, at once, shake the dust of Gales Hill and all its environs from my feet this very second.

I saw no one as I crept silently out of the house. It was still dark. I thought I heard a slight movement in the garden as I passed through it but I paid little heed. It was a rabbit, I supposed, or some bird that moved in the bushes. For once there was no wind. The air was still and heavy as though with thunder approaching. Sure enough, I had gone only a short distance when the first flash of lightning streaked across the sky and a crash of thunder tore through the silence. I set off to run, and managed to reach a small wooden shed close by the roadside, as the storm broke.

As I sheltered there my thoughts flew at once to Jimmy. He was terrified of thunder, especially if it came by night. We had suffered a severe storm a little over a week ago, and the next morning when Polly came to bring my hot water, she had found the boy asleep, huddled up outside my door. For some strange reason, the nearness to myself must have somehow lessened the poor creature's fear. I wondered if he would act in the same way now and come creeping down the attic steps and on to the front landing, unaware that my chamber was empty.

The storm over, I set off again. I walked, meeting no one, to the railroad station where I had first arrived. The porter remembered me and addressed me by name as he bid me good morning. There I boarded the train for York. It seemed the best place to make for until I could make some definite plans for the future.

Without too much difficulty I found a cheap lodging-house fairly near to the station. Worn out physically and emotionally I took off my outer garments, lay down upon the iron bed and fell fast asleep.

For two days I tramped the city's narrow streets, looking in vain for some employment. I had a little money left from my dress allowance but I knew it would not last very long. Weary and dispirited I was about to enter my lodgings at the close of the second day, when two men approached me. They asked if my name was Helga Radford and when I replied in the affirmative, announced they were officers of the law. Their faces were alien and unfriendly, and a feeling of dread assailed me. What now, I asked myself despairingly? What further blow could life have in store for me? Too terrified to speak I waited for them to explain their business with me. They told me I was wanted for questioning in connection with a murder: the murder of my grandmother!

What followed was like a nightmare, a hideous dream from which I felt I should never awake. I was arrested, taken to the police station and charged with murder. In vain I protested my innocence. In vain I wept and pleaded. Almost out of my mind with terror I was dragged down a flight of steps and into a prison cell. It was indescribably filthy and the stench almost made me vomit. In a space meant to accommodate perhaps fifteen people, some twenty to thirty were crowded together, rough evil-looking persons of both sexes. Some of them were drunk. Others stared at me.

As the heavily barred iron door clanged behind me, a surge of blinding panic overcame me and I turned and banged on it frantically with my fists. I clawed at the unyielding iron until my hands were torn and bleeding and until a woman, less evil-looking than the others, dragged me off and into her corner of the cell. There was one window, only a fraction of which was above ground level. From it I could see the feet of passers-by. Through its bars, filth from the adjacent fish market trickled into the cell. There was no light and no washing facilities. One pewter utensil served for the bodily needs of us all. Hell itself, I decided, could not be much worse. Then mercifully a kind of stupor descended upon me. Numbed with shock and despair I fell into a trance-like state, at times only half aware of my surroundings. It was, I suppose, my mind's way of dealing with something it found too monstrous, too terrifying to face or endure. I longed for the complete escape that sleep would bring, but such respite was denied me. Crouched in my wretched corner I sat, stiff and cramped, unutterably weary yet sleepless, through the long suffocating hours of darkness.

Next morning I was offered a pint of coffee and a hunk of bread for breakfast, but I pushed them away. To have eaten and drunk anything would have choked me. Shortly afterwards I was bundled out of the cell, up the steps and taken in a sort of cart to the railway. Nobody told me what was happening or where I was going. Two men, one of them one of those who had arrested me, accompanied me. Once we had boarded a train he explained that I was being taken back to the East Riding where I would be held in custody to await committal proceedings there. Not really comprehending what he meant, I again protested my innocence of any crime, but I could see by the men's faces that they did not believe me. They had already made up their minds that I was guilty.

A terrible despair threatened to overcome me, but one thought and one alone, kept me from going under. I *was* innocent. If, as they said, Grandmother had indeed been murdered, the deed had not been committed by me. Somebody else had killed her. But whom? And why? For the life of me I could find answer to neither question. Why should anyone want to kill my Grandmother? Of all the people around her, and I presumed it must be one of these, no one it seemed to me had any reason for doing so. None of them had anything to gain from her death. Francis indeed had every reason to wish her alive: she had been going to change her will back in his favour. If as the men said she had been murdered on the night I left home, the will would still be in *my* favour. Fear rose in my throat...I and I alone had had motive for wanting her dead...

Too proud to weep in front of the men, I fought back the tears of helplessness that threatened to overcome me. Oh, I thought achingly, if only Edward or dear Papa were here to help and advise me. I felt so alone, so friendless and yes, although I was half-English, an alien. I understood nothing of the processes of law and such ignorance heightened my terror. Thinking about Papa reminded me that I still had Grandmother's letter to him in my reticule. Just for something to do I took it out to read it again. And as I unfolded the paper something that had baffled me fell into place. *The writing was the same as in the anonymous letter. This* was where I had seen it before! But who had penned that letter on behalf of my blind grandmother? That was what I had to discover. The vicar had read Papa's letter to Grandmother, he had told me so, but he had said nothing about replying to it on her behalf. Mrs. Lewis and Lavinia had been in Europe. There were the servants of course but none of them could read or write. That left one person. Francis. Francis had written that vile, poisonous letter about me himself. I felt myself go white with anger at his treachery. One of the men asked if I was ill but I shook my head and said I was all right. I was sick enough, sick to my stomach, but it was not the sort of malady that he could do anything about.

The train clattered on and I began to agonise afresh as to who the murderer could be. I had established Francis as the anonymous letter writer but that did not bring me closer to discovering the identity of Grandmother's killer. Or did it? I sat bolt upright on my hard seat as an idea came to me. To have stooped so low, Francis must need the money badly. Supposing he needed it *now?* Hope surged within me. He could have a motive after all. The will was still in my favour, true, but if I were to be hanged for murder, then it would go to him at once. He would not have to wait for Grandmother to die...The more I thought about the idea, the more convinced I became of the truth of it. He had heard me say, in front of the others, that I could kill Grandmother, had realised what motive I had and had seized his opportunity...But how was I to prove it? With sinking heart I knew I had not the remotest chance of doing so.

How many days I was in custody I do not remember. My nerves almost at breaking point I seemed unable to keep account of the passage of time. Sick with fear and tortured by the waiting, I became so weak and ill that when I was finally brought before the magistrates, I could hardly stand.

In a daze of blinding despair I heard the facts of the case and the evidence against me. Grandmother had been shot, while sleeping, on the night that I had fled from Gales Hill. She had been shot at close range, through the head. The weapon had not been found, but the shot had been fired from a pistol like the one I had brought to the house a short time ago. I had quarrelled bitterly with my grandmother, had been heard to say I could kill her...I had everything to gain from her death...As I listened I could almost feel the hangman's noose about my neck...my head ached abominably and my heart hammered suffocatingly against my ribs...Then all at once a door behind me was flung open. Pandemonium broke out as someone strode into the room and approached the magistrates. I watched as in a trance, my eyes glazed with misery. Then a wave of nausea swept me and the blood began pounding in my ears. I clutched out vainly for support as the room and everyone in it started to spin around me...When I regained consciousness I was told that I was free. New evidence had been uncovered which had cleared me completely.

Later, at the vicarage where I was to make my home until Edward returned, I learned what had happened.

I owed my deliverance it seemed to Jimmy, the idiot boy. It was he who had led them to the real murderer, Mrs. Lewis.

'Mrs. Lewis? But that is unbelievable.'

The vicar sadly shook his head.

'I'm afraid it is true,' he told me. 'It is a most grievous and distressing story.'

'And where is she now, Sir?'

'Dead, by her own hand.' I asked about Lavinia and learned that she was being cared for by friends. Then the vicar told me how the truth had come to light. Although no one could be sure exactly what had taken place, it would appear that Jimmy had witnessed something, something that had a disturbing effect on him. For after the night of the shooting he had started to behave most strangely. The servants had found him time after time in one of the bedrooms on the first landing, somewhere he had no business to be, and he seemed to be looking for something. When they had dragged him away each time, he had become upset almost to the point of violence. He had gesticulated wildly and tried desperately to tell them something. At first the servants had attached little importance to his odd behaviour, but then one day he had managed to get out the word 'gun' and they began to have second thoughts. So they had mentioned the matter to Francis but he had dismissed it airily on the grounds that the boy was an idiot. They had wanted to tell Mrs. Lewis but she had been confined to her bed, suffering from shock, Lavinia said, since the tragedy, and was not to be disturbed. Polly had told her mother and she in turn had mentioned it to him, the vicar. He, believing all the time in my innocence, had thought there might be something important behind the lad's story.

'I always felt,' he went on, 'that poor Jimmy had more sense in his head than most people gave him credit for, and I decided something should be done. A thorough search was made of the bedchamber, and in a secret drawer of the dressing-table we found a pistol.'

'But that proves nothing,' I objected.

'Something else was in the drawer,' the vicar said slowly. 'A diary. In it was a confession to your grandmother's murder.'

He had gone at once, that night to Mrs. Lewis's bedside and confronted her with it, had informed her that he would be presenting it to the magistrates the next morning.

Lavinia had found her dead later that night. An empty poison bottle told its own story. She must have had it hidden somewhere in her room ready to be taken if her crime was discovered.

The diary revealed everything, even to the reason for keeping it at Gales Hill and not in the Dower House. That room had once been my father's and to her it was a sort of shrine. Emma, as she then was, had worshipped Papa and until my mother had appeared on the scene had been sure he would marry her. She had at once planned to kill Mama and had feigned friendship with her in order to get an opportunity to do so. The plan had been to invite 'Fraulein' on an outing to the coast and then push her over the cliffs in some lonely, isolated spot. She, Emma, would then say that Fraulein had tripped and fallen, and nobody would doubt her word. But my grandparents had forbidden the outing and also any association whatever with 'the foreign governess from the Hall,' and so her plans had been thwarted. Papa and Mama had eloped, and she had been left, heartbroken and alone. In her pride she had never let Papa see for one moment that she thought of him other than as a brother.

'No one, according to the diary, suspected her true feelings,' the vicar continued. 'No one.'

'I think one person did,' I said slowly. 'Two in fact.'

And I told him of the old couple at the lodge with their stares and talk of trouble.

The vicar nodded.

'Servants see more than is sometimes realised,' he agreed, and then went on with the story. In her bitterness and loneliness, Mrs. Lewis had begun to turn against my grandparents. She loved them in a way, the diary revealed, but with part of her mind she blamed them for her unhappiness. Their unrelenting opposition to 'the German woman' had not only prevented Emma from getting rid of her, but had also precipitated the elopement of the two lovers.

'When the letter telling of your own birth arrived, she tore it to shreds and burned it. Mad with jealousy and rage she was determined to keep from them news that she knew might have pleased them.' So Papa's first letter *had* arrived after all. I asked how Mrs. Lewis had got hold of the letter before my grandparents, and was told that according to the diary she had always taken charge of the mail as soon as it arrived. Suddenly I realised what it was that I had heard one day, months back, and had failed to see the significance of. It was Lavinia saying something about her mother telling her that she, Lavinia and I, were *about* the same age. Deep down in my subconscious I must have wondered how she knew how old I was.

'There was of course a further reason for her destroying the letter,' the vicar was continuing. 'She could not bear the thought of seeing your parents together, happy and in love; she knew that the letter just might bring about a reconciliation. She also realised that any chance of killing your mother with your father always by her side, was now extremely remote.'

She had married the elderly Mr. Lewis a month afterwards, openly admitting in her diary, that she had no love for him whatever. His fortune was what she wanted. She had hated me on sight. At first just because of my mother, but later also because of Edward. I was doing to Lavinia what my mother had done to her. She decided as before, to pretend friendship for me, then to await her chance and kill me as she had intended to kill Mama. In my case however she planned to make it look like suicide if possible, and that was why she had stolen the pistol from my drawer earlier on. Francis had played into her hands by bringing about the quarrel with Grandmama: it was in just such circumstances that my death by my own hand would be accepted unquestioningly. She had suffered a bad moment when I had declared my intentions of leaving Gales Hill immediately after the quarrel, but having managed to persuade me to stay while morning, had crept down, as planned, to murder me as I slept.

Furiously angry and frustrated that I had escaped her, she had in a flash of devilish inspiration seen how she could still destroy me: she would kill Grandmother and I would take the blame. The sordid story was finished at last. I shuddered. But for Jimmy and his fear of thunder, for I was certain he must have seen Mrs. Lewis while creeping down the steps to my door, her fiendish cunning would have succeeded...

EPILOGUE

Edward came home within a week of my being set free. I had been through blackest hell. With his return I entered Heaven. As he enfolded me in his arms and embraced me I knew that everything was going to be all right. He was furiously angry when he learned of my ordeal, and berated Francis, the poor vicar and the magistrates roundly for not having contacted him. He would, he avowed passionately as he held me close, have swum the Channel if necessary, to come to my aid had he known of my plight.

He was scathing in his condemnation of Mrs. Lewis, but after a while I persuaded him to feel slightly more merciful towards her. She had been an embittered woman, I pointed out, a woman whose loneliness and disappointment had perhaps unhinged her brain a little. She was deserving of pity as well as disgust.

We were married just as soon as the arrangements could be made. Lavinia was my bridesmaid. She is married herself now, to the penniless tutor, and the two live in London, the place Lavinia always longed to be. There is no shortage of money for she has, naturally, inherited her mother's fortune. It did not take her long to recover from the effects of the tragedy. She showed a resilience which surprised me. I miss her, but all in all it is better that she has moved away.

I, of course, inherited Gales Hill and the bulk of Grandmother's wealth, neither of which I desired. The house and most of the money I made over to Francis. I felt that he had more claim to them than I had in spite of his foul behaviour. He came to me one night before Edward returned and begged my forgiveness. He confessed that he himself had made up the slander about me. All that Polly had said to him was that Bessie was heartbroken because I was 'sending' Jason away, that they both wished I had never come to Gales Hill. I myself had told him about the bright farm lad who stayed longer than the rest. Mrs. Lewis had told him of the night I came in with the pistol, and, as I already knew, about the Graham-Lewis episode. There was enough to concoct a convincing story to put before Grandmama, he had decided. Mrs. Lewis had agreed.

'I swear I wouldn't have done it but for the gambling debts,' he pleaded. 'Without the prospect of the old girl's money, ruin stared me in the face.' I did not find it too difficult to forgive him for I truly believed that although his behaviour had been low and contemptible, he had acted more from weakness and fear than from downright wickedness. He had known nothing of Mrs. Lewis's plan to murder me.

Swearing eternal gratitude to me for being 'such a sport' about everything, Francis quickly disposed of Gales Hill and moved South. Only when he had left the county did I dare to tell Edward what he had done to me. Had I done so earlier I was sure he would have killed Francis with his bare hands. As it was I had difficulty in preventing him from following 'the low, unspeakable bounder' and thrashing him with his horse whip.

The rest of Grandmother's money we have put in trust for Jason. He is doing well with his music and from the letters he write to us is obviously very happy in Germany. Some day, he will be famous, I feel certain of it. Bessie, I hear, is being courted by a farmhand.

Edward and I of course, live at Southwold Hall. Jimmy, bless him, is installed in one of the attics there. He will always hold a special place in both our hearts.

One or two little things still puzzle me. I never found out, for instance, why Grandmother asked the vicar to read her Papa's letter instead of waiting for Francis. In my own mind I have the idea that she had begun to mistrust Francis slightly, but it may have been merely impatience, for she certainly chose him to reply to it for her.

As regards the hints she made about Mama's character, I shall never discover what she meant, and it could well be that I was over-sensitive and that she meant no more than she made out, that she was just showing a mother's natural concern for her son's happiness. Perhaps she had heard of Mama's quick temper and worried on account of that...The more I think about my mother's outbursts, I have come to the conclusion that there was nothing behind them and that it was just her impulsive nature. Edward says so anyway. He says that most impulsive people are quick-tempered, both he and I for example!

The lodge couple no longer stare. They smile at me now and the old woman drops a curtsey. I have not spoken to them of Mama or of Mrs. Lewis, and I do not intend to do so. I am trying to forget all that happened, and for the most part it is only in my dreams that the past returns to haunt me. But sometimes when I am out riding alone and I catch sight of the chimneys of Gales Hill I remember everything... And in my mind's eye I see a picture of a lonely, embittered woman writing behind a locked door by the light of a candle, a woman half-insane with passion for revenge, writing in her diary of her plans to murder me...

And upon such times I turn my horse and ride as fast as I can back to Southwold Hall, to the joy and sanity of the present and the bliss of my husband's arms.

This Large Print Book for the Partially sighted, who cannot read normal print, is published under the auspices of

THE ULVERSCROFT FOUNDATION

THE ULVERSCROFT FOUNDATION

. . . we hope that you have enjoyed this Large Print Book. Please think for a moment about those people who have worse eyesight problems than you . . . and are unable to even read or enjoy Large Print, without great difficulty.

You can help them by sending a donation, large or small to:

**The Ulverscroft Foundation,
1, The Green, Bradgate Road,
Anstey, Leicestershire, LE7 7FU,
England.**
or request a copy of our brochure for more details.

The Foundation will use all your help to assist those people who are handicapped by various sight problems and need special attention.

Thank you very much for your help.